# AN INVISIBLE CLIENT

# OTHER TITLES BY VICTOR METHOS

# AN INVISIBLE CLIENT

## VICTOR METHOS

THOMAS & MERCER

Published by Thomas & Mercer, Seattle

www.apub.com

Amazon, the Amazon logo, and Thomas & Mercer are trademarks of Amazon.com, Inc., or its affiliates.

ISBN-13: 9781503952768
ISBN-10: 1503952762

Cover design by Ray Lundgren

Printed in the United States of America

*To Noah. My hero.*

*Justice will not come until those who are not injured are as outraged as those who are.*

*—Solon, 560 BC*

# 1

Food manufacturers have a formula to determine whether we should live or die.

I sat at the plaintiff's table inside a courtroom at the Utah County District Court in Spanish Fork, Utah. A vice president from Bethany Chicken was on the stand, testifying. I stared at him, wondering what he'd thought when he first heard the formula. Was he shocked? Did he try to fight it? Was he apathetic? At some point, he decided to succumb. He may have been a good man before that. A family man. A God-fearing Christian man. A charitable man. One decision changed that, and he became worse than any drug dealer or pimp my firm had ever defended.

The formula was simple. It was based on one that a judge named Learned Hand—his actual given name—had written in a legal opinion, probably unaware what the implications were. The food industry had run with it.

Defects in food—bacterial infections, rot, mold, cross-contamina-tion with allergens, exposure to toxic substances, and everything else that could go wrong—were discovered by manufacturers long before the general public knew. The manufacturer then had a decision to make: do we recall the food or not?

Actuaries worked out death tables that predicted how many people would die or become ill because of the defect. They could determine how much money the average person who bought the product earned per year: that person's earning capacity. Adding up the earning capacity of everyone who could potentially die or get sick because of the defect gave them an estimate of how much settlements would cost. Under the law, a consumer's value equaled the amount of money that person could have earned in a lifetime, had he or she lived. If the calculation of damages in all the wrongful death lawsuits was greater than the cost of a recall, the manufacturer would recall the product. If the settlements would cost the company less than the recall, then they just ignored the defect.

*Damages > Profit = Recall*

Every bite of food we eat is like rolling a pair of dice. At some point, somewhere, someone was coming up snake eyes. And that's when they would seek me out.

This time, the snake eyes came up for my client's seventy-one-year-old husband.

The judge, an elderly man who had recently lost a hundred and ten pounds after having his stomach stapled, still wore his extra flesh like a deflated balloon, and the excess skin on his cheeks bunched up when he spoke. But he was about as gentlemanly a judge as one could find in Utah County.

"Your witness, Mr. Byron," he drawled.

I rose slowly and buttoned my suit coat. At the defense table sat the corporate defense attorneys—a litigation firm hired by Bethany Chicken's insurance company, in-house counsel for Bethany Chicken, and a defense litigator from the insurance company itself. Five attorneys at one table.

The only people at my table were me and a seventy-year-old widow in a yellow dress. I was one-third partner at a firm with twenty lawyers. I could have had people there, too, but I wanted to be the underdog. I wanted the jury rooting for me.

Normally, I wouldn't have taken this case. The deceased's earning capacity wasn't high enough to make my fee worth the time commitment. But the widow was so sympathetic that I knew a jury would eat out of her hand when she testified. She couldn't even mention her husband's name without crying. The more tears she shed up there, the higher the dollar amount of the award in the verdict.

I stepped to the lectern. Barry Harper, a bald man wearing a Rolex watch, had worked at Bethany Chicken for ten years. His immaculate gray pinstriped suit was not unlike my own. But I wore a blue tie and a blue pocket square because our jury focus groups had said jurors responded best to blue.

"What's the Black Test, Mr. Harper?" I asked. I never stood behind the lectern. I always stepped to the side. If possible, I stood right in front of the witness, but some judges didn't allow that.

"I have no idea."

"You don't know what the Black Test is? That's your testimony?"

He nodded. "I don't know what that is, Mr. Byron."

"No idea what the Black Test is, correct?"

"I've told you twice now, sir, that I don't know what it is."

I grinned. "And we can trust you on that, can't we?"

He paused, as if wondering where the trap was. "I'm telling the truth, if that's what you mean."

"You're telling the truth because if you did know what the Black Test was, and you got up there and said you didn't know what it was, well, that would be perjury, wouldn't it? Which is a felony."

"I don't know the law."

"But you know that to lie under oath in a court of law is a crime, don't you?"

He thought that over. "Yes, I believe it is a crime to lie under oath. I don't know the degree of that crime. But I'm telling the truth."

One of the defense attorneys, a pasty-complexioned man named Rosenberg, stood and said, "Objection, Your Honor. We've established that Mr. Harper is telling the truth. What exactly is the purpose of this line of questioning?"

"Getting there, Judge," I said.

"Get there a little quicker, Mr. Byron."

I put my hands behind my back and took a few steps toward Harper. I stopped and looked at him. I looked him right in the pupils for a long time, long enough that he began to fidget. I walked back to the plaintiff's table and picked up a sheet of paper I had set out. Turning back to Harper, I pretended to read it silently.

"So if I had an email written to you on June fourteen of this year at 2:07 in the afternoon, by a member of your staff, that said a recall of unit 4379 didn't pass the Black Test, and you replied with 'OK,' there would only be one conclusion we could draw, wouldn't there? That you have just lied."

"Objection!" Rosenberg screamed. "Plaintiff's counsel has not provided any such email to the defense. I would vehemently object to its introduction and ask that this be argued in chambers."

I smiled at the judge. "I haven't moved to introduce it yet, Your Honor. We can have that argument when I do."

"Objection overruled."

I took another step closer to Harper. His cheeks were flushing red now, and I had to suppress a grin. I could almost hear his internal dialogue: *Who the hell wrote that email and didn't delete it? Would I be so dumb as to respond to that?*

"A felony, Mr. Harper," I said loudly, waving the paper around as though it were the Bible. I stepped right up to him, standing close enough to smell his cologne. "A felony."

"Objection, Your Honor. This is—"

"It's not worth it, Mr. Harper. It's only money. Don't go to jail over it. What is the Black Test?"

"Judge!" Rosenberg was yelling now. "He is attacking my witness as though—"

I enunciated each word: "What. Is. The. Black. Test?" I waved the paper in front of him.

Harper swallowed, looked down to the floor, and said, "It's an actuarial exercise."

I could've heard a pin drop in that courtroom. Or in the case of Bethany Chicken and its insurance company, I could have heard six million dollars, which was the amount of damages we were asking for. I looked back at Rosenberg, who collapsed in his chair and groaned loudly enough for everyone to hear.

"An actuarial exercise," I said, taking a step back and looking at the jury. I went up to the whiteboard I had asked the bailiffs to bring out. I uncapped a marker and wrote *Damages > Profits = Recall.*

"That's the Black Test, correct?"

"Yes," he mumbled. He couldn't even look at the defense table.

"It means that if the settlement of lawsuits and the damages you have to pay out on defective food is greater than the profits you make from that food, then you issue a recall. Right?"

He nodded.

"Please answer me audibly, Mr. Harper."

"Yes."

"So let's just say your actuaries tell you ten people will die from bad eggs, and it would cost you a thousand bucks per lawsuit to quiet that, but you're only making five thousand in profits total. Then you would issue a recall. Correct? To save that additional five-thousand-dollar difference."

Harper poured water out of the jug at the witness stand into a paper cup. He took a sip and looked to Rosenberg, who was leaning back in the chair. Rosenberg tossed his pen onto the defense table as though it were a towel in a boxing ring.

"Yes," Harper said.

"But there's a flip side to this equation, isn't there?" I wrote on the whiteboard the formula: *Damages < Profits = No Recall.*

"That's an accurate statement of your business practices, isn't it, Mr. Harper?"

He was playing with his lapels and looking at the defense table. He couldn't look at the jury. "I don't know."

"Well, look at it. If the damages are higher, you recall. That means when the damages are lower, you don't recall. Simple logic, isn't it?"

"I . . . I suppose."

He was a blubbering mess. Cheeks so red that he suddenly looked sunburnt. He knew the enormity of what he'd done. The consequences for him would be swift and severe. Whoever Bethany was, I guessed she didn't put up with people who couldn't handle five minutes of questioning.

"It's already been shown to this jury that you learned about the salmonella in unit 4379 on February second of this year, two weeks before the death of Jason Hardaway. This wasn't negligence, was it?"

"I don't understand the question."

"I said, this wasn't negligence, was it? You knew what would happen, but it was cheaper for you not to recall and just pay a few pennies to people like my client. People whose husbands and sons and mothers and sisters died because you wanted to save a few bucks. Money over mercy, right?" I did love my soapbox.

Rosenberg finally stood up, and I was surprised he hadn't done it sooner.

"Your Honor—"

The judge cut him off. "I know, I know."

"Your Honor," I said. "I believe Mr. Rosenberg would like to take a ten-minute break to speak with me."

The judge shrugged. "Let's make it fifteen."

I walked past the defense table and laid down the sheet of paper face up. It was an email confirmation from a Las Vegas hotel stating I had booked a room last month. Rosenberg sighed and crumpled the sheet.

# 2

The Spanish Fork District Court sat in the middle of a field. A few homes and the high school ringed the western edge, but three sides looked out on open desert. The entire front of the courthouse, both floors, was nothing but glass, where we could sit and watch people riding dirt bikes at the sand dunes a little farther out.

Rosenberg sat down on the bench across from me. He rubbed the bridge of his nose. My partners, Marty Keller and Raimi Val, leaned against the hallway wall. They had watched only a couple of hours of testimony. As partners, we didn't really have to go to trial. Our associates could do it all. I was the only partner who still preferred to fight it out himself. Neither Marty nor Raimi was particularly good in a courtroom, but that wasn't why I'd joined up with them. Marty's empathy toward potential clients and Raimi's research skills, talents I didn't possess, complemented my trial prowess.

"What do you want, Noah?" Rosenberg asked.

"You read the complaint. Six million."

"That's crazy, and you know it. The guy was a year from retirement, and he was a mechanic. He wouldn't have made six million if he'd worked the next two hundred years."

Raimi, Marty, and I had decided we would settle this case for anything over five hundred thousand dollars. Given the deceased's earning capacity, that would be more than fair.

"Two million," I said.

"Still too high."

I leaned forward. "Did you not hear what just happened in there, Glen? Your boy just lied to the jury. I'm gonna spend the next hour going through every single thing I can think of with him. He's so flustered, he'll probably tell me the times he jerked off to dirty magazines as a kid. And then, when I put my client on the stand—oh, Glen, when I put my client on, there is not gonna be a dry eye in the courtroom. Her husband was her entire life. Nothing else mattered."

Rosenberg glanced toward the attorney–client meeting room next to the courtroom, where the other attorneys and representatives of Bethany Chicken had gathered. "Let me talk to my clients."

He rose, went into the room, and shut the door. I looked back at Raimi and Marty and winked. My client came out of the bathroom and slowly walked over to where I was seated. She sat down with a groan, leaning on the cane I'd insisted she bring to the trial. Her ankles looked swollen and purple.

"I think you're about to become rich, Claire," I said.

She grinned. "That's nice."

"What're you going to do with the money?"

She would get a nice chunk of the money, but it wouldn't be anywhere near the full amount. Personal injury attorneys took thirty-three percent of any settlement, and if it went to trial, the fee got bumped up to forty percent. That was after expenses were reimbursed for things like investigators, mediators, stenographers for depositions, photocopies, phone calls, and court filing fees. The best scenario was the one I was in—to settle the case on the first day of the trial. If I could settle today, I would still get the forty percent and I'd save myself two weeks in court.

"I'm not keeping any of it," she said.

"Leaving it to your kids?"

"Oh, no. Well, I'll put some aside for my grandchildren's college, but the rest, I'm giving away. This wasn't about money for me, Mr. Byron."

"Ma'am, no disrespect, but it's always about money. No exceptions."

She smiled a sad little smile. "You'll come to find as you get older that money loses its luster, and the only thing that matters are the people in your life. Nothing can bring Jason back to me, but maybe I can make some other people happy with this money."

Clearly, she and I did not come from the same school of thought. I was about to ask her something else when, out of the corner of my eye, I saw two bailiffs—younger guys—standing around with dopey grins on their faces. When I looked down, I saw what they were staring at.

A small mouse padded along near the wall. It was gray and somewhat fat, with little whiskers that twitched every so often. A baby. The bailiffs had laid out a spring trap with chocolate, and the baby mouse was headed for it.

I rose and went over there. Both bailiffs looked at me but didn't say anything. I took my pen—a Montblanc I had picked up for fifteen hundred dollars—out of my pocket and tapped the spring on the trap, setting it off. The baby mouse heard the noise and scuttled in the opposite direction. I stood up, eyes on the bailiffs, then sat back down.

Rosenberg stepped out of the conference room and hovered by the door, away from my client. I guessed he didn't want to see that she was a real person in actual pain. I walked over to him, and he whispered, "One point two. Expires in ten minutes."

I grinned and held out my hand. "You're reasonable. That's why I like you, Rosenberg."

"Yeah, I'm sure that's what you tell everyone."

---

The drive back to Salt Lake City from Spanish Fork took an hour. Raimi rode with me. I liked driving with him because he didn't talk much. He was the most brilliant lawyer I had ever met, but he couldn't sign a client to save his life. His social skills had never really developed past high school, and I had always presumed he fell somewhere on the autism spectrum. I brought it up with him once, and he'd hinted that because his parents were Hindu they believed disabilities were not disabilities but gifts from the gods.

"You hungry?" I asked.

"No. There's a new law clerk you need to approve in the next few days. BYU grad, top ten in her class."

"You know I don't give a shit about grades. They don't mean anything."

"They mean they're the type of person to get good grades in law school. Probably the type of person who would work really hard for us."

I hadn't gotten good grades in law school. In fact, I'd nearly flunked out, and only by the grace of the relationship I had built with the dean of academics over the years was I allowed to graduate. Law school was a sham, but every student blindly believed in that sham. Schools didn't teach anything lawyers would actually use; they proclaimed the law was a noble profession and couldn't be sullied by teaching practicalities like marketing, sales, entrepreneurship, and client management. But the jig was up. Graduates had become less and less employable as the market flooded with lawyers, and law school applications were down nearly fifty percent from ten years ago. People were getting the message. Practicalities were the only things that really mattered.

"The top-ten people are kinda weird," I said.

"Weird how?"

"I don't know. What kind of weirdo forsakes their family and social life to sit in a library and study ten hours a day?"

"I did that."

A beat of silence passed. "You sure you're not hungry?"

"No."

# 3

The offices of Byron, Val & Keller occupied the fifteenth floor of the Salt Lake Mercantile Building. We had twenty-three attorneys and forty support staff. When Raimi, Marty, and I started the firm, we'd had five thousand dollars among the three of us and only two desks. In ten years, we'd become one of the top plaintiffs' personal injury firms in the state.

Our firm had grown to handle family law and bankruptcies, as well, but I didn't touch that stuff. I did do some criminal defense. It wasn't that much different from personal injury: a big faceless machine bearing down on an individual with all its might. The worst odds of winning a case were in criminal defense and plaintiffs' personal injury. Lawyers who wanted to win had to be selective, particularly with PI, where the lawyers fronted the costs of the case. Picking only winners was important, because one crap case could bankrupt an entire law firm. I'd seen it happen when attorneys grew emotionally attached to a case—the cardinal sin of personal injury—and paid the price by investing all their money and eventually losing.

The firm across the hall had taken out a four-million-dollar loan on a medical malpractice case they'd thought was a sure thing. Even though the doctor had been drinking before the surgery, the jury found that there was no negligence on his part—juries could never be trusted to do the smart thing—and the bank called in the note. The firm couldn't pay, and I'd watched the bank take apart the firm piece by piece and sell everything from the lamps to the computers. One of the partners, a portly man named Nick, had stood in the hallway and cried the entire three hours it took to move the furniture.

Raimi and I opened the glass double doors to our office and walked in to applause and cheers. The secretaries and paralegals had a tradition of baking a cake with my face and dollar signs on it when we settled a big case. They wanted to put the things I valued most on there, and Raimi had told them it was money and ego. Not too far off the mark, I guess. It wasn't money itself that I cared about, but what it represented: freedom, power, and luxury . . . all tied up in one neat little green sheet of paper.

Our office manager, Sally, whom the staff called Commandant because she was so strict with them, raised a hand. "Quiet." She leaned in to give me a single kiss on the cheek, then lit the lone candle on the cake. "For keeping us all employed."

I blew out the candle and made a wish.

Then I headed to my office, the largest office here, with floor-to-ceiling windows that looked over downtown Salt Lake. On my way, colleagues slapped my back and shook my hand. We had made about five hundred thousand dollars, which was nice, but that wasn't a massive payday. I think they were more excited because they knew I gave out bonuses whenever we had a decent settlement, and they were hoping that by treating this as a large settlement, they would get a little piece of the pie.

A year ago, I had settled a ten-million-dollar suit for three million and took everyone in the firm to Hawaii. I wouldn't be doing anything like that for five hundred thousand dollars, but a few bucks wouldn't be a big deal.

Sally followed me into my office, helped me take off my suit coat, and hung it on the rack in the corner. I sat down behind the glass-and-steel desk, and she took her spot across from me.

"Give everyone a thousand-dollar bonus," I said. "And send Rosenberg a bottle of champagne."

"He's Mormon. He doesn't drink."

"Rosenberg's Mormon?"

She shrugged.

"Okay, well, send him a basket of bread and honey or whatever."

"Done. Next?"

"The Katz case, the blind guy who ran into the branch hanging over the sidewalk, any word from the city?"

"They want to talk resolution, but it looks like they're not offering much."

"It's not worth much, but it's a slam dunk. The city let the tree grow over the sidewalk and should've known people would run into it. Let Marty take that—he knows the city attorneys better than I do—but tell him I want at least a hundred thousand. The guy's got scars all over his face that should get us to that."

She wrote furiously on her legal pad. "Next?"

"Our billboards on I-15 look like crap. They're all covered in dirt. Get someone from Kennedy Billboards out there to clean them."

"It's not dirt. It's buildup from the smog."

"Can they be cleaned?"

"Yes."

"Then have 'em do it today."

"Okay, done. Anything else?"

"Get me a latté, would you?"

"No prob. Oh, your ex-wife called. She'd like a call back."

I rolled my eyes. "She wanna borrow money?"

"Wouldn't say."

"I'll call her later. I got anything on my calendar today?"

"Nope. You're blocked out for the next two weeks for trial."

I grinned. Another benefit of settling cases at trial was that I would officially be out of the office until the last day of trial. "I'm going to the gym, then."

"Your gym clothes are hanging in the closet."

"You're the best," I said, standing.

"I know. Call your ex-wife. No woman likes to wait for a phone call."

I grabbed my gym bag and started taking off my tie. "I'm sure it's nothing important."

# 4

After the gym, I headed back to the office for an afternoon consult—a referral from another attorney who felt the case was too complex for him to handle. A skinny man with glasses came into my office and sat down. He began telling me about a car accident. Within minutes, he was crying—not tears but a blubbery crying, like a child about to leave Disneyland.

I knew within two minutes that I wasn't going to take his case. The fact was, the law was a harsh mistress. People liked to tell themselves they were unique, that everyone was special, and his or her value couldn't be measured. Well, the law didn't see it that way. Under the law, a person was valued at exactly how much money that person could earn. Anyone who hadn't gone to an Ivy League school, pulled in at least six figures, or had a family business waiting for them was what PI lawyers called "an invisible client"—one who lived and breathed but didn't officially exist.

We didn't take invisible clients. The solo practitioners could fight over them.

After five minutes, I stopped him. "Mr. . . . James, is it?"

He nodded.

"Mr. James, I'm very sorry for the situation this other driver has put you in, but we can't take your case."

"Why not?" He looked absolutely shocked. Most clients I turned away had the same look, and it surprised me every time.

"Because liability is far from clear. You rolled through a stop sign, and he ran a red light. Not good facts for either of you."

"But . . . the pain. I'm in pain every day. I can't sleep at night. I can't watch TV. I can't go out . . ."

"I know, and I'm sorry, but the value of this case is just not very high. The loss of your income isn't as high as I would need to take the case when liability isn't clear. It's true that pain and suffering and your medical bills are important, but those numbers don't add up to much. I'm sorry—you just don't earn enough."

His face flushed pink, his lips pursed, and he stood up. "Well, you are a rat sonofabitch, aren't you?"

He left my office, and I took a deep breath and leaned back in the seat. It was six in the evening. A few associates were still running around the office, but most of the staff had gone home. In an hour, I would hear the vacuums of the cleaning crew.

I headed down to my reserved parking space, got into my Bentley, and drove about two miles uptown to a wine bar called Gleam, where I had the valet park the car. Raimi and Marty were already at a table. This was one of our traditions, too: get trashed the night of a big settlement and find some beautiful women to spend the evening with.

"Gentlemen," I said, sauntering up to the table, "what are we drinking?"

"Just wine for me," Marty said. "I've got a date."

I sat down. "What the hell are you talking about?"

"I got a date with Penny."

"So cancel."

"I can't cancel. It's getting serious with her." He paused. "I think I might ask her to marry me."

Raimi kind of twitched, his version of excitement. "That's stupendous. Congrats."

"Marty," I said, putting my elbows on the table, "what the hell are you talking about?"

"I think it's time. I'm sorry, Noah. I love going out with you guys—you know that—but I'm getting older. Maybe it's time to hunker down. I know it wasn't for you, but I think it could be for me."

Marty's parents were older and had lived through the tail end of the Great Depression. Seeing them keep old newspapers for toilet paper and reuse the same grease for every meal for a week had influenced him more than he'd ever admit. Made him crave safety over risk, even when it wasn't to his advantage. We'd gone to Las Vegas once and he bet a five-dollar chip, lost, and then skipped dinner that night to make up for it. Living the bachelor life was too much of a gamble: wait too long for the right person, and you could end up alone.

Marty, though, hadn't seen the disadvantages of marriage. The slow separation that began like a crack in an iceberg. The marriage would splinter somewhere and both of you would be holding on so tightly you couldn't breathe. Some people saw the fracture and still stayed married. They were the ones who sat quietly in restaurants and didn't speak or look at one another. Other couples, like me and my ex, couldn't stomach the thought of living a life with a person they no longer loved.

I leaned back in my seat. "What's your favorite breakfast cereal?"

"What?"

"Breakfast cereal. Like Lucky Charms, Fruity Pebbles, Wheaties, what?"

"Um, I dunno. Cinnamon Toast Crunch, I guess."

"Cinnamon Toast Crunch? Do you eat it every day?"

"No."

"No, of course not. Why?"

He shrugged. "I'd get sick of it." He rolled his eyes. "A woman is not a cereal, Noah."

"Same principle, man. Why would you tie yourself down to one woman when you can be with a different woman every night?"

"Because I love her."

I chuckled. "Love is a creation of advertising, Marty. It exists only in your head."

"Well, aren't you a ray of sunshine today. I thought you'd be happier for me as my best man."

I sighed. I was being a bit of an A-hole. "I'm sorry. I'm really happy for you. Really. Penny's a great girl." I raised a finger in the air, indicating to the waitress that I was ready to order. "Now let's get smashed."

---

Raimi drank very little and could drive, but I was slurring my words and hitting on every woman in the joint. We headed outside and said bye to Marty, whose girlfriend had dropped him off. I had secured myself a date for later, but decided I wasn't in the mood. Marty's news had thrown me off more than I would admit to anyone.

Raimi drove me home. I lived at the top of a mountain near the University of Utah. We stopped in the horseshoe driveway, and I said, "Make sure to get my car from the valet."

"I'll get someone from the firm to drive it. Leave your garage open." His nose scrunched up in a puppy-dog way. A tick he sometimes got when he was about to say or do something uncomfortable. "Are you really happy for Marty, or did you just say that?"

"I don't know. Happy. Whatever. How come you don't drink?"

"I don't like the feeling of not being in control. I like to control everything I can. I don't like taking risk."

"You opened this firm with me. That was a pretty big risk."

He shook his head. "No, it wasn't. I knew you'd make us successful. It was a good bet."

I grinned. "I think that's the nicest thing you've actually said to me, Raimi."

"You're welcome."

I slapped his shoulder, then got out of the car.

"Hey," Raimi said through the open window, "call Tia. She texted me and said it was important."

"She still has your number, huh?"

"I was the one she would call to find out where you were at three in the morning."

He had said it without any malice, just stating a fact, but it felt like an accusation. Maybe my own guilt was bubbling to the surface.

"She was a good woman, Noah."

"She still is. Have a good night."

"You, too."

I turned to my home, stood in the driveway for a minute, then decided I wasn't yet drunk enough to call my ex-wife.

# 5

The home had three levels, each set up for different purposes and with a different atmosphere. On the bottom level were the pool table, the weight room, the projection screen, my library, and a small bar. The middle level was where guests came and ate and marvelled at the view. The top level with the balcony was only for me. I had never taken anyone else up there.

I got out a Guinness and drank down half before walking out onto the balcony. From there, I could see all the way from the mountains in the east across the valley to the mountains in the west. I took another sip, then sat down in a lawn chair. The house was quiet, and the neighborhood, just as much. I'd grown up dirt poor. Every day, getting enough to eat had been a challenge. Living in a neighborhood like this—without the sounds of screaming couples, bass thumping in passing cars, and children playing outside at all hours—had a calming effect I'd never experienced while growing up.

My phone buzzed in my pocket. I took it out. Tia. I let it ring a few times, staring at her name on the screen.

"Kinda late to be calling, isn't it?" I said. "People might think you still have a thing for me."

"Since when have I cared what people think?"

"You care what your mother thinks."

"You love my mother and care what she thinks, too."

A slight twinge of guilt hit me in the gut. Her parents had taken me in and treated me like a son, and in exchange, I'd treated their daughter like crap. I'd stayed out long hours, missed holidays . . . One birthday, I left her present unwrapped on the counter. When I came home, she was crying on the couch. I'd sat down next to her without a word and we stared at the walls. I think both of us knew that night it was over, though the marriage lasted another six months. We both cared about the other so much, we were willing to stick it out as long as we could just to spare the other one's feelings. A situation that was corrosive to the soul in a way few other things were.

The morning after we separated, she had her brothers come pack her things. She moved to Los Angeles, where her parents lived, and I hadn't seen her since.

I remembered the last time I had kissed her. It was odd to think about, that there was a last kiss. It happened in the car. I dropped her off at work and said good-bye and we kissed. I remembered the scent of her lotion and the trace of her lipstick. I still felt it sometimes on my lips, like a ghost limb from some part of me that had been cut off.

"How's your mom?" I said after too long a silence.

"She's okay. They're thinking of moving to Florida."

"That cliché? At least choose Palm Beach or St. George or something."

"They have friends in Florida. My dad's plan is to become a tour guide."

"Has he ever actually been to Florida?"

"Not once."

I chuckled. "He'll make a good guide, then. I bet he'll just make stuff up that sounds entertaining." I looked out over the city. "The lights keep multiplying every year. They reach a little farther over the mountains and a little higher into the trees. Salt Lake'll be a big city soon. Don't know if I wanna stick around for that."

"Please. You're a big-city kid. You'd be so bored in a small town, you'd cause trouble just to stir things up." Silence lingered between us, then she said, "I called for two things, Noah."

"Yes."

"Yes, what?"

"Yes, you can borrow money. Just email Jessica what you need, and she'll—"

"I don't need money, you jerk. Just listen to me . . . I'm getting . . . I'm getting remarried. We're doing it in Hawaii sometime in the winter. Haven't set an exact date yet . . . Noah, you still there?"

I thought about this house. It had been our dream to own a home like this, but when we were married, I wasn't rich yet. We were barely making ends meet, shopping at dollar stores and taking out payday loans just to buy some food and pay the electric bills, using candles when we'd maxed the loans we could get. We'd come to neighborhoods like this and look at the homes and I would make grand promises about how ours would be bigger than any of these, and she would live like a queen. She'd kiss me and tell me she believed that I could conquer the world.

The first night I spent in this house, alone, the only thing I could think was that I wished like hell she could see that I'd made good on my promise.

"Yeah, yeah, I'm here. Sorry. Um, well, that's great news. Richard, right? Works for a nonprofit or something?"

"Yes. He asked me yesterday, and I said yes. I wanted to tell you before you heard it from someone."

I took a deep breath. "You don't owe me any explanations. You deserve those mansions I promised you. I'm glad you found someone who can do that for you."

"That's a relief. I thought you might be upset."

I shook my head, though there was no one around. "No. No, I'm happy for you. I'll bring a nice gift to the wedding."

"Richard and I talked, and we think that maybe . . ."

"Oh. Yeah, that would be awkward. No big deal. I'll send something."

"Thank you for being understanding about this."

I wanted to throw the phone across the lawn, but instead, I said, "Well, I better go. Got a hot date."

"Just one more thing. I was wondering if you could do me a favor?"

Anger rose in me like a ball of heat. Tia had just told me she was getting remarried, and now she was asking for a favor in the same call? She must've really thought I was a sucker.

"What?" I asked.

"My cousin, Rebecca, her boy is really sick. It's from that whole Pharma Killer thing. He was one of the ones who took it."

I knew what she was talking about. Everybody did—it had been all over the news out here. Some psychopath had laced children's cough medicine with cyanide. Three kids in Salt Lake County had gotten extremely ill, but none had died.

"Sorry to hear that, but I don't know what I could do. They haven't caught the guy. And even if they did, he wouldn't have any money. It's not worth it."

"I know, but her boy is really sick. He's only twelve. It would make her feel better if she met with you. She's got a lot of anger and just needs someone to listen to her."

"Tell her to hire a shrink. That's not my job."

A beat of silence passed.

"Okay, Noah. I'll tell her. Sorry to bother you so late."

"No, wait. Wait. I'm sorry. Just a long night. Have her call the office and set an appointment. I'll meet with her. But make sure she knows there's nothing I can do. I don't want her crying in my office when I tell her no." I reached for the beer, which I'd put down and it tipped over, the black fluid bleeding into the wood of the balcony. "There's a lot of other personal injury attorneys you could've called."

"You're the best at what you do. I know that."

An entire life flashed before me just then. A life with her. Kids and grandkids. Birthdays and graduations. But that wasn't my life now. It was for Richard.

"Night, Noah. Take care of yourself."

"Yeah, you, too."

---

I woke up still on the lawn chair. The sunlight blinded me for a moment, and I squinted, then covered my eyes with my hand. Once my eyes adjusted, I rose and looked out over the city. A thin gray haze stuck to it like pus. I went inside, showered, and changed into a navy Armani suit with a white shirt, a red tie—to show assertiveness—and a red pocket square. The Bentley was back in the garage, and I drove it down to the firm.

It was past ten by the time I arrived, and the firm was buzzing with activity. Luckily, because I was officially supposed to be out, none of that activity was directed at me. I went to the break room, fixed a cup of coffee, got a banana out of a fruit bowl, then sat down in my office and stared at the reflection of the city in my computer screen.

I'd been born and raised in Los Angeles. When I'd moved here, Salt Lake City had been about as different from LA as Mars was from Earth. Now they had begun to resemble each other. I meant what I'd said to Tia last night: I wasn't sure I wanted to stick around for that transformation.

"Sir," my secretary said over the intercom.

"Yeah?"

"Rebecca Whiting here to see you."

"Who is that?"

"A consult. I placed it on your calendar with notes. She's your ex-wife's cousin."

"Oh, right."

"She wanted the soonest appointment available. I knew you didn't have a trial, so I set it for this morning. Hope that's okay."

"Yeah, it's fine. Send her back, would you, Jessica?"

"Sure."

A moment later, my office door opened, and Rebecca Whiting walked in.

# 6

Rebecca didn't look familiar, though I was sure we'd met before. She had brunette hair and crystal-blue eyes. She hadn't dressed up, which was unusual because most potential clients did. She wore sweats and no makeup. Her eyes were puffy, and her hair was pulled back and held in place with an elastic band. I rose and shook her hand.

"Thank you for coming," I said.

"We've met once before, Mr. Byron."

"Call me Noah." I sat down. "Where?"

"At a wedding with Tia for my other cousin, Sandy."

"Oh, right," I said, still not remembering.

"I'm sorry you guys didn't work out. I really liked you. You were nice to us when you met us."

I had made some kind of impression, and I was glad it was a good one. I wasn't known for controlling my drinking at weddings.

"It's all right. I'm glad Tia's found someone."

She nodded, staring at a gold penholder on my desk. "Did she tell you what this was about?"

"Yeah, your son is sick. Is that right?"

She nodded. "Joel. He's twelve. Just turned twelve. Do you know about Herba-Cough Max? The kids' medication?"

"I've heard about it. Someone laced it with cyanide, if I remember."

She nodded again. "That's the story. That some lunatic laced children's cough medicine with poison. But that's not what happened. Not what I think happened, anyway. There's more to it."

Her eyes started to glisten. She was fighting back tears, and I got the impression that it was taking everything she had not to break down right there.

"What makes you say that?" I asked.

She took a tissue out of her purse and dabbed at her eyes. "I talked to them. They're covering up. Someone from their company, Debbie Ochoa, told me they were the ones that started the rumors about a lunatic. She told me that on the phone. I'd gotten to know her because I would call so much, and she told me that. Now they tell me she isn't there anymore."

"Where were you calling?"

"Pharma-K. They're the company that makes the medicine. They got all these kids sick, and now they're covering it up."

"Do you have any proof other than Ms. Ochoa's statement?"

"No. They won't talk to me anymore. Just transfer me to their attorneys, who don't tell me anything. I tried to go to the news, but they wouldn't listen. They think I'm crazy."

I'd seen horrific accidents befall children, and without a doubt, the most common reaction from parents was disbelief. To have someone to blame—someone to point the finger at and say, "They did this"—was so cathartic that if that person didn't exist or if the parents didn't know who it was, they would invent him. I had a feeling that was what

Rebecca Whiting was doing. Her boy had been one of the unfortunate ones to suffer because of some sick maniac, and without the maniac, she needed to blame someone. Pharma-K was as good a choice as any.

"Ms. Whiting," I said softly, "I'm not sure what you'd like me to do."

"I want you to sue them. Sue them so they can never hurt another child again. They're just gonna keep doing this if they think they can get away with it."

I tried to be as compassionate as possible. "So, let's assume you're right, that this is something they're covering up. That means the police investigation would have to be flawed, or maybe the police would have to be in on the cover-up. Dozens of employees of the company would have to know what was happening and agree to keep their mouths shut, and the investigative journalists working this story would have to come up with nothing in support of this view, or again, be part of it. All those things would have to happen for this to be true."

To her credit, she held my gaze. I continued. "But for us to win a lawsuit, all of those things would have to be true, and we'd have to be able to prove it in a court of law. I don't see how exactly we would do that without spending tens of thousands, if not hundreds of thousands, of dollars."

"Money? Is that really what this is about?"

"It's always about that."

"My son is dying, Mr. Byron. He's in renal failure. The cyanide wasn't enough to kill him, but it was enough to ruin his kidneys. He's on the transplant list, but he's too sick. I thought the transplant list was for sick people, but if they're too sick, they don't get a kidney. They'd rather give it to someone who has a higher chance at survival."

She dabbed at her eyes again. I didn't know what to say. She was asking me to take on a case that we would likely lose.

"I'm sorry. I don't think our firm can help."

She sniffled. "Will you talk to them? Pharma-K? Just go out and talk to them. See what they say. My boy's at the university hospital, and I'm there all day and night if you talk to them and then want to meet with us. Please, just talk to them." She hesitated. "I knew no lawyer would take this case, but Tia said you would look at it. That you wouldn't just turn us away like everyone else."

Her eyes held a desperation that I'd seen only a few times in my life: I was her last resort.

I clenched my jaw, as if preparing for a blow, then slowly relaxed. "Okay, I'll talk to them."

---

Jessica set an appointment with Pharma-K for six in the evening, and by five, I was actually itching to leave the office, but I didn't want to go home. So I told myself the meeting would be a nice little distraction. I would joke around with the executive, maybe have a drink or two, and down the line, maybe he would even think of me if he had a case he wanted to send out.

Marty came to the door. "Hey, I heard about that Pharma-K thing. You really thinking of taking that case?"

"No. I just told the client I would meet with them."

He put his hands in his pockets and strolled into my office. "Might not be a bad idea to take a look. The company's probably terrified right now. They might settle a suit just to get rid of us."

"Why would they possibly do that? I would fight tooth and nail if I were them."

"You're not them. They have shareholders who get spooked easy. Cyanide in their children's cough syrup is spooky. If there's anything there, it might be worth exploring. If nothing else, it would get us some press. This Pharma Killer story is everywhere."

For some reason, I was annoyed that Marty thought the case was a good idea. "Do you know how much we would have to spend? Just on investigators and depositions alone, it would probably be two hundred grand. Maybe more."

"Oh, probably more, but we would take the first settlement and run. I'm just saying, if it seems like something they'd settle after we look into it, we should consider it."

"I'll think about it."

"Okay," he said, nodding. "Oh, almost forgot, that interview's here."

"What interview?"

"Raimi was supposed to tell you about her. BYU grad—he wants her in the bankruptcy division?"

"Shit. Just freakin' hire her. What do I need to interview her for?"

"We agreed that all three of us would interview new hires, no matter how big we got. Has to be unanimous. One for all and all for one."

I chuckled. "You're such a dork."

He shrugged. "I gotta be me. I'll send her in." He turned to walk out, then said, "If there's anything there with Pharma-K, I might seriously consider it."

"I said I'd think about it."

# 7

When Olivia Polley walked into my office, I was reading the CV Raimi had sent over, but only to see what her hobbies were. No other part of a CV said as much about someone as what they thought others should know they liked to do. I'd seen everything from "stand-up comedy" to "exotic dancer." I'd interviewed the exotic dancer and left the comic alone—too much gloom and doom in those people's personal lives.

Olivia looked younger than me and wore glasses. Her chestnut-brown hair skimmed her shoulders. She shook my hand, smiled widely, and said, "Hi," in the way a teenage girl might say it. "I recognize you from the billboards."

"That's my twin, actually."

"Seriously?"

"No."

"Oh," she said, as though she didn't understand I was joking.

"So Raimi is really impressed with you. He thinks I should hire you. Do you think I should hire you?"

"Yes . . . wait . . . yes?"

"It's not a trick question."

"Oh, then yes. Yes, you should hire me."

"Why?"

She swallowed. Her face flushed a light hue of red. "Um . . . I don't know." Immediately, she mumbled, "Dang it, that was so stupid."

I chuckled. "At least you're honest. Look, I have nothing to do with our bankruptcy division. That's Raimi's thing. I only do PI and occasionally criminal defense. You're going to be in Raimi's division, so if he wants to hire you, I won't stand in his way."

She sat there for a long time, staring at me.

"That means you're hired," I said.

"Oh, thank you. That's great. I'm so excited. I'm sorry for being such a goon. This is my first interview."

"Your first interview for a lawyer position, you mean?"

"No, my first interview ever."

"*This* is your first job interview ever? You never had a paper route or waited tables or anything?"

She shook her head. "No. Mr. Val and Mr. Keller did their interviews on campus. It was group interviews, so this is my first real one."

"Well, good for you. The working man gets screwed, so it's good you've never had to put up with it." I looked at her CV. "So, in your spare time, you play chess, huh?"

"Yeah, I have senior master status. I was the first woman in Utah to do that. I love the game."

"I used to play, too. Gave it up, though. I don't remember why."

"I can start right now," she blurted. "I mean, you know, if you need someone who can start right now, I could."

"You're already hired."

"I know, sorry. I read an article about how to do job interviews, and it said to make sure you say you can start right away."

I stared at her for a second, then chuckled. "Okay, well, you can start right now . . . actually, hang on."

I stepped out into the hallway and poked my head into a few offices. I didn't want to go down to Pharma-K by myself—it was always best to have at least one witness for this sort of thing—but it looked like I'd waited too long. All the associates had gone home.

"I do need your help right now, if you're ready," I said, walking back into the office. "Just need a warm body to come with me and listen in."

"Sure, I'd love to. Where are we going?"

"To see where the sausage is made."

---

I had Olivia drive while I researched Pharma-K on my phone. They weren't a massive drug company—their annual revenue was at about two hundred million—but they were gaining market share. They had been founded in New Jersey but moved to Utah in 2001 for the tax rebates. If a company had above a certain number of employees and agreed to hire local workers for a certain percentage of future openings, they could set up shop in the state of Utah essentially tax-free.

The most unique thing about the company was what they termed their "Pharma Future" program, a division of the R&D department that hired the top minds graduating from pharmacy schools and chemistry programs around the world, and dumped money on them to come up with new drugs. One article I looked at estimated that, because of the drugs being worked on in Pharma Future, the company would triple in value over the next five years. All the profit tax-free.

"Working man really does get screwed. He busts his ass for thirty grand a year and pays twenty percent in taxes, and a company that's making hundreds of millions a year pays zero in taxes."

Olivia, whose hands were turning white from gripping my steering wheel so hard, said, "It's not their fault."

"Whose, the working man's?"

"No, the company. Everyone would pay less in taxes if they could. It's the government's fault."

"And who do you think sent attack-dog lobbyists to Washington to get their taxes so low?" I scrolled through a portion of another article. "Don't tell me you're a libertarian?"

"Sort of. Are you?"

"Yeah, I'm all for state-of-nature, dog-eat-dog philosophy, but you struck me as the bleeding-heart liberal type."

"I'm some of that, too."

Pharma-K's headquarters were in a section of Davis County known as North Salt Lake City, though the area was actually a completely separate city from Salt Lake itself. North Salt Lake had been founded by the owners of a mining company who thought they could get more hours from their workers if the miners didn't have to drive back to a different city at the end of the day. The town consisted almost entirely of factories, warehouses, and manufacturing plants, with a few fast-food restaurants thrown in for good measure. A constant haze of thick, soupy smog hung over the surrounding county. It sometimes blew over the rest of the valley and made the air nearly unbreathable. I had once walked around wearing a surgical mask, and when I took it off at the end of the day, the mask was brown.

"Right here," I said.

"Pharma-K? Is this about the Pharma Killer case?"

"It is."

"Whoa."

"And by the way, as an employee of Byron, Val & Keller, anything you see and hear is confidential. Don't tell anyone about anything you see on the job that could be confidential, okay?"

"I won't."

We parked in front of a modern-looking business park, all steel and glass, with a courtyard in between three identical buildings. The grass was well kept. I always looked at the grass in front of buildings. When a property was struggling, they cut the landscaping budget first.

Pharma-K took up the top half of the first office building, floors three through six. Their manufacturing plant occupied a separate building. Inside the polished chrome elevator, I watched Olivia take a hit from an inhaler. We got off on the sixth floor and walked into the vestibule ahead of us.

A woman who looked like a model sat behind the large desk, smiling widely. "Hi, guys, how can I help you?"

"I have a meeting with Darren Rucker."

"Okay, hang tight one sec. Okay?"

She remained quiet, the smile still on her face, and I realized she actually wanted a response. "Sure, we'll wait."

We sat down on the orange leather chairs. This didn't look like any drug company I'd ever seen. Electronic music played over the speakers, and quotes from people like Nikola Tesla decorated the walls.

A man came out of an office down the hall. He wore jeans and a sports coat and sunglasses pushed up into his hair. He smiled and shook my hand. "Darren, COO of Pharma-K. You must be Noah."

"I am. This is my associate, Olivia."

"Oh, very nice to meet you." He kissed the back of her hand. She blushed.

He looked back at me. "Everyone's in the conference room."

"Everyone? I thought this was just a chat between us."

"Just a few people. Nothing big."

We followed him down the hall. The office walls were primarily glass, and one large space was crammed with cubicles. We passed a break room that held a Ping-Pong table and an arcade video game I didn't recognize. Off to the side was a massive conference room.

An oblong crimson table, with at least thirty yellow high-backed chairs around it, took up the room. About ten of those chairs were filled.

Darren said, "These are our lawyers. I think you know Bob there."

I knew Bob. He was senior partner at Walcott, Smoot, Bagley & Hockett, one of the biggest law firms in Utah and Nevada. They catered exclusively to corporations with gross revenues higher than fifty million, and billed at an hourly rate of five hundred dollars, an obscene amount for the Mountain West.

Bob was in his sixties and had once been the Utah State Bar president. An eye patch disguised his allegedly blind left eye. The gossip, which no one had been able to verify, was that he didn't need the eye patch and had himself started the rumor about being blind. Supposedly, he just thought the eye patch made him more intimidating.

His deposition tactics had put him on the radar of every plaintiffs' personal injury firm. During depositions, he would excuse himself to the bathroom, leaving the plaintiff's attorney alone with his or her client. Upon returning, Bob would demand to know everything said between the attorney and the client while he was in the bathroom. Opposing counsel would protest that their conversation was covered by attorney-client privilege. Bob, a smirk on his face, would then point to the stenographer in the corner. The presence of a third party negated attorney-client privilege, and everyone always forgot the stenographer was there.

I'd encountered Bob on my first big personal injury case and fell for his trick.

"I heard you got a nice settlement from Bethany Chicken."

"No complaints," I said, sitting down. This was clearly an ambush. In addition to Bob, there were at least four other lawyers in the room. "So I thought this was just going to be a friendly chat with your COO here. I didn't realize the troops were marching."

"Oh, it is friendly," Bob said with a grin. "I'm always friendly."

We stared at each other for a moment.

"So," Bob said, "what should we talk about?"

"I'd like to talk about cyanide, Bob. Namely, how it got into your client's cough medicine."

The room fell silent. A few of the lawyers exchanged glances. They were scared of something. They seemed to have been hoping I'd come about something else.

"Tragedy," Bob said. "Thank goodness nobody was killed."

"I got a visit from a little boy's mother yesterday. She thinks he might not make it."

Bob shook his head. "Damn shame. What's this world coming to when lunatics go around poisoning children's medicine, for heaven's sake? My clients just can't believe it happened. They're doing everything in their power to help the families of the victims and working with law enforcement to bring that sick bastard to justice."

"Seems weird, though, doesn't it? I mean, if I were a sick maniac— and I'm not, but if I were—I'd want to poison different types of cough syrup. Not just one brand from one company, in one geographic location. That's too easy to take off the shelf."

The lawyers glanced at each other again, but Darren Rucker just stared at me.

"Listen," Bob said, "you've been doing this, what? Ten years? I've been defending companies for thirty-six years, son. And I can tell you, this company has done everything in its power to help the victims of this tragic situation. We set up an emergency board that met every day until the emergency was taken care of. We donated money to the county so they could devote more police officers to finding the man who did this; we issued a recall on the product; we—"

"Why a man?"

"What?"

"You said 'finding the man who did this.' Why a man? Why not a woman? What makes you think it's a man?"

"It's just a figure of speech, son." He grinned. "See," he said to everyone in the room while still looking at me, "Noah here is a little insecure. When I was at Harvard, we got a lot of that. People who just didn't make it and carry chips on their shoulders. I think you went to school somewhere in the Midwest, didn't you?"

"University of Kansas."

He nodded. "So you still have a little bit of that Ivy League chip on your shoulder, don't you?"

I had to swallow to keep my anger in check. "We both have the same law license, Bob. I paid twenty grand for mine. You paid ten times that for yours. Who's the sucker?"

Bob ran his tongue along his upper lip, like a predator that had just seen prey. "Someone decides to get medicine down off the shelf and poison it. That is not my client's fault, and you're wasting our time."

"Bullshit!" Olivia blurted.

Everyone in the room, including me, stared at her. Instantly, her eyes went wide, and her cheeks flushed red.

Bob said, "Looks like your associates still need to be housebroken."

"My associates can speak their minds. Go ahead, Olivia. What do you mean?"

She swallowed, and her lower lip quivered. I thought she might pass out. "I was . . . I was watching *Ellen* and . . ."

"Excuse me," Bob said, "did you say *Ellen*?"

"Yeah. And they had a pharmacist on. One of the families bought the cough syrup from a pharmacy."

"So?" Bob said.

"So the pharmacy buys it directly from the manufacturer, already sealed. Then they stock it near the front at that pharmacy. There's cameras there. No one could've tampered with it without someone seeing them. It had to come from the manufacturer with the cyanide already in it."

I stared at Bob, who looked over at Darren.

"Well, Bob? Response?"

Bob rose. "Let's talk in private."

He put his arm around me and walked me out into the hall, away from earshot of the others.

"Listen, I know where you're going with this. I know all about it. But it's a dog case. Do you know what Pharma-K's revenue will be this year? Four hundred million dollars. More than double what it was last year. This is a company that's on the rise, and they will do anything to protect their reputation, spend any amount of money. You're getting into a war you can't win."

My tie was slightly askew. He adjusted it and said, "Go back to the playground. You're not ready for the big boys, counselor."

As he walked away from me, I said, "There's blood."

"What?"

"There's blood in the water, Bob. If I had shown up and talked with Rucker for a few minutes, I would've left and told that woman there wasn't a case here. But you brought out an army. There's blood in the water and I can smell it from a mile away. You made a mistake. It'll be interesting to learn what's got you so spooked."

I stepped away from him and poked my head into the conference room. "Let's go, Olivia. We're done here."

# 8

We pulled out of the lot and got onto I-15 heading back to Salt Lake. Neither of us spoke until we were getting off the freeway downtown.

"That was weird," she said. "They were totally scared."

"I know. But that doesn't mean we can prove anything. They might just be scared about the bad press a lawsuit would bring. It was weird how quickly the wagons circled, though." I exhaled loudly. "How is it you've never had a job?"

She glanced at me. "My mother is really ill. Schizophrenia. She's been sick for as long as I can remember. I needed to stay home and take care of her when I wasn't at school, so jobs and friends and stuff were never really an option."

"How'd you guys survive?"

"I got her on disability, and I would knit stuff at home, caps and scarves, and sell them on Etsy. That would make ends meet, usually."

"How'd you pay for law school?"

"Knitted a lotta fucking scarves."

I laughed. She laughed, too, a soft, pleasant sound.

"We got one more stop before heading back to the office."

---

The hospital wasn't far from my house. It sat up on the side of the easternmost mountains in the valley, surrounded by shrubbery and trees. We parked near emergency parking. I guessed that Joel Whiting would probably be in the ICU, so we headed there.

The receptionist directed us to a room at the far end of the corridor. I saw Rebecca in the corridor, heading into the room, and when she saw me, her face lit up.

"Mr. Byron. You came."

"Noah is fine, Rebecca. Hope we're not here at a bad time."

"Not at all. One second." She tapped on the glass window of the door, then whistled, two loud whistles. She waited a second, and two whistles responded from inside the room. I gave her a quizzical look. She smiled. "When Joel would get lost at a park or something, that's how we'd find each other. So we use it now to let each other know where we are. It's silly."

We sat down on the chairs against the wall.

"Tell me what happened that day," I said.

She stared off into space. "I was in the kitchen, loading the dishwasher, and Joel came in from playing baseball. That's his favorite sport. He came in and threw his glove onto the table, and I told him to move it. He started coughing. He'd had a cough for a couple of days, but I knew he didn't like doctors, so I didn't take him in. It was just a cough." She bit her lower lip. "So I got the cough medicine down from the kitchen cupboard that I'd bought earlier. It was in a little purple bottle. He argued, like all boys do, but he did as I asked. I gave him two capfuls, the recommended dose, and he seemed fine. He got a juice out of the fridge, went into the living room to watch television . . ." She was silent for a long time.

I said, "What happened next, Rebecca?"

She bit her lip again. "He, um . . . I didn't hear anything. So I went into the living room to see what was going on . . . and I found him on the floor. He was just flat on his stomach, like he couldn't move. I ran over to him, and I was shaking him and screaming his name, but the only time he moved was when he vomited." She wiped the tears away from her cheeks. "I called 911, and then I just held him. I didn't know what else to do. I just held him."

I waited until she was ready to speak again.

"Anyway," she said, "the ambulance came, and they took him to the hospital. They thought he'd had a stroke. And then they told us they thought he'd had a heart attack. They didn't know what to look for. And then a nurse said she'd heard of another little boy across the valley who had gotten sick after taking this cough medicine that had cyanide in it. So the hospital tested the medicine, which they were nice enough to go to my house and get so I could stay with Joel, and it came back as having cyanide in it. But not a lot. Just enough to hurt a child."

Tears started flowing again, and she took a few crumpled tissues out of her pocket and dried her eyes.

"We've been here ever since. His kidneys are failing. The cyanide wasn't enough to kill him. But it did a lot of damage. They won't give him a transplant. I've tried everything to convince them, even called the governor's office, but they won't do it."

"Is there a chance he'll recover?"

"I pray for that every day. But according to the doctors, no. He's getting worse every second."

I couldn't believe they wouldn't get him a transplant. Several of my clients had received transplants, even alcoholics and drug addicts who would get clean just long enough to test and qualify for the organ. It didn't make sense that they wouldn't give a kidney to a little boy who'd done nothing wrong.

"So," she said, "did you talk to them?"

"I did."

"And?"

I chose my words carefully. "It was . . . odd. If the COO had just met me, apologized, and said he was doing everything he could to make the situation better, that probably would've been the end of it. But they had a team of lawyers there. It was like they were trying to scare me away."

"I knew it! I knew they were hiding something."

"That doesn't mean they're hiding anything. They could just be frightened of the bad press from a lawsuit."

She shook her head vigorously. "Mothers know these things, Noah. They did this to my boy, and they're trying to get away with it."

"Where did you buy the medication?"

"At a grocery store, Greens. It's by our house. A little store just in the neighborhood."

"Did you check the tamper-resistant seal?"

"Of course. It was sealed. No one had tampered with that bottle. I'm sure of it."

I rubbed my forehead. "Do they still have the bottle, in case we want to retest it ourselves?"

"I guess the police would. They came and took it." She stole a quick glance through the glass on the door. "So, are you going to help us?"

I looked at Olivia. She wore the same pleading expression that Rebecca did.

I couldn't take the case yet; liability wasn't clear and I didn't want to jump in until I knew for certain something was there. But it wouldn't hurt to look. "I'm not officially taking the case, but I'm going to look into it a little more. Maybe send out our investigator and see what he can turn up."

She smiled and put her arms around me in a hug. Surprised, I didn't move. Though Rebecca didn't look much like Tia, something about them was similar. Just a scent, maybe, or the way their touch felt. It sent a jolt through me. When she pulled away, I stood and said, "I'll be in touch for some more information tomorrow."

"Don't you want to meet him?"

I glanced toward the door. "Sure."

# 9

Rebecca whistled at the hospital room door. Two whistles responded. She opened the door, and I followed her into a private room filled with balloons and flowers. Olivia came in behind me and leaned against the wall. In front of me, a particularly large balloon proudly displayed the San Francisco Giants logo, and a Giants jersey, white with red trim, hung on one wall. I cast my eyes over these things before I turned to the bed.

Joel Whiting was abnormally thin for a twelve-year-old kid. His arms and legs were like sticks. His pale face had lips so cracked he looked like he'd been lost in a desert. The dark circles under his eyes stood out like makeup, and even though he looked dehydrated, his face was puffed up, as if he were retaining too much fluid. He wore a San Francisco Giants baseball cap.

"Joel," his mother said, "this is Mr. Byron. He's a lawyer. He's going to be helping us."

"Hi, Mr. Byron," he said, voice as soft as the squeak of a mouse.

"Hello, Joel."

I didn't know what to say. I had no experience with children. One of my ex-girlfriends had had a son, but he'd been just a baby. I could place a baby somewhere and not have to interact. This boy was full-on staring at me, expecting something. It made me uncomfortable, and I had to look away and clear my throat.

"Giants fan, huh?" I said.

"Yeah. My daddy used to take me to their games. I saw them play the A's, and we got popcorn and sodas." He seemed equally as excited about the popcorn and sodas as the game.

"Must've been fun."

"Do you like baseball?"

"Not really. Boxing was always more my sport."

"Oh," he said, disappointed. "My mama won't let me watch boxing. She says it's for people who are violent."

Rebecca blushed, though I didn't feel insulted in the least.

"That's true. Your mother is a smart lady."

"Look at this," Joel said.

He reached over to the small table by the hospital bed. The effort it took seemed gargantuan, but he slowly wrapped his fingers around a card and held it up for me to see. I took a step closer.

"It's a Barry Bonds card. It's not a first edition—those are really expensive—but my daddy got me this at Giants Stadium." He turned the card around and stared at it, seeming suddenly sad. "He hit a home run when I was there, and my dad wanted to catch it, but it was too far away."

I nodded. "That's a cool card. I would hang on to that. It's gonna be worth something one day."

"Who's that?" he said, looking at Olivia.

"Hi, Joel," she said, approaching the bed. "I'm Olivia. I work for Mr. Byron. And guess what? I love the Giants. I lived in San Francisco for a summer."

"No way."

"I did. I even went to a few of their games, and I saw them beat the Oakland A's, too."

"I hate the A's."

"Me, too," she said softly, as though they were sharing a secret.

In her interview, she had seemed shy and socially awkward, but around Joel she softened. As though the edges of her personality had been taken off and only the core remained. It was easy to tell she was someone who loved children.

He looked at the card. "I'd like to go back again."

I heard a knock behind us, and two nurses brought in a machine I hadn't seen before.

"Hey, Joel," one of them said. "It's that time again, buddy."

"Already? I was talking about the Giants with Mr. Byron and Olivia."

"Mr. Byron and Olivia can come back when we're done."

Rebecca gently touched my arm. "It's time for his dialysis. We should go."

"It was nice meeting you, Joel."

"You, too, Mr. Byron. Bye, Olivia."

I saw the nurses get the needles ready, and I couldn't watch. We went out into the corridor again, and his mother looked back through the small glass window above the door handle.

"He's on hemodialysis," she said. "Four times a week. The needles are painful, but the worst part is the muscle cramps. He gets really bad muscle cramps, and I'll just stay and massage him for hours."

I put my hands in my pockets and glanced at Olivia. "He's a good kid."

"The best a mother could ask for. It just doesn't seem fair that we don't get enough time together. But I thank the Lord every day that we get this time together, right now. Just me and him."

"Where's his father?"

"His father died in Iraq. He was a JAG officer. They hit his jeep with a rocket, and he died last year."

"I'm sorry."

She glanced at me. "The Lord sent you here, Mr. Byron. He sent you here to help us and make sure that no one else's child has to go through this."

A dying boy, who's as American as apple pie. What jury could resist him? Even if liability wasn't clear, if I could get Joel into that courtroom and put him in front of that jury to talk about the pain he'd gone through . . . to tell the jury about the needles they had to stick into him four times a week and how he probably can't sleep and has nightmares . . . The jury might give me whatever I asked for. Bob would understand that, too, and probably pay us to make it go away.

"I don't know anything about what the Lord wants," I said, "but I'll help you if there's a case there."

---

"How are we going to get Joel to the court to testify?" Olivia asked while I drove us back to the firm. "I once read a case in law school where the judge and jury came to someone's hospital room. Are we gonna do that?"

I shook my head. "Nine out of ten cases don't go anywhere near a jury. Pharma-K will probably settle to keep it away from one."

She was silent for a second, then said, "That's why you might take this case, isn't it? It's not to help them."

"First rule of being a lawyer is that it's always about the money, Olivia."

I stopped the car in front of our building to let her out.

"I guess it will help them. Any money they win, I mean." She opened the door and slid out. "Thank you," she said. "I'm glad I came."

"Hey," I said. She leaned back in through the open door. "You shouldn't blurt things out at meetings. You tip your hand that way, rather than being able to use it later. But thanks, the tip about the pharmacy was good."

She smiled shyly. "You're welcome. So I'll see ya around the firm, I guess."

"Actually, I was thinking. Raimi doesn't need another bankruptcy associate right away. But I need someone in PI if you want. You passed the Bar yet?"

She grimaced, her nose scrunching and glasses rising above her brows. "Couple months. July. I've been studying eight hours a day. If you're worried I won't pass . . ."

"Not worried. Think you can handle studying and the work I'll throw at you?"

"Yes. I mean, I would love to."

"Okay, nine a.m. tomorrow. I'm going to have a meeting with our investigator about this case. I want you there." I grinned. "I know you can start right away."

# 10

I had set a meeting with our investigator for nine, but I was in the office at eight—the earliest I'd been there in years. Olivia arrived early, too. She was wearing a light blue suit, and she stood at my office door until I said, "You can come in."

"Oh, thanks." She sat down across from me.

"How's your mom?" I asked.

"Good. I told her I was hired here. I think she was happy. Didn't really say much about it."

"Did she not want you to become a lawyer?" I thought of my own father; the only thing he ever said about lawyers was that he wished he could get a hunting license for them.

"My grandfather was a chemist, and I think she thought I would go into the sciences. The thought of just being in a lab all day made me crazy, though. I want to be out, making big arguments to judges to change the law."

I chuckled. "The law is like a big rusty ship. You can't change its course without nearly destroying the ship in the process."

I noticed her looking at a spreadsheet attached to a file on my desk. I slid it toward her. "Take a look. Make sure my numbers are correct."

She flipped through the demand letter—a brochure created for insurance companies, outlining the damages to my client and the amount we were seeking. Her eyes scanned the document so fast I wasn't sure she was actually reading. Taking a pen off the desk, she clicked it and then marked up the document.

"The estimate for long-term care is wrong. It says for eleven years and five months but it's only calculated for eleven and three months. That should be an extra four thousand."

"Four grand in thirty seconds of work. I should have you come in here more often."

She blushed a little and set the file back on my desk. "I feel bad for Joel. He lost his dad last year, and now he has to live in a hospital. Doesn't seem fair."

"Whether or not something's fair isn't the right question for us. The question is, how much is the case worth? You might not like that, but this family didn't come to our firm so we could hold their hands. They came to get money for their suffering."

"Mrs. Whiting doesn't seem like she cares about the money."

"Yeah, everyone says that until I hand them a check with a lot of zeros."

My intercom beeped, and Jessica said, "Sir, KGB is here."

"Send him back."

"KGB?" Olivia asked with a raise of her eyebrows.

"His name's Anto. He's Serbian and was in the special forces. Marty's an idiot and didn't realize Serbia and Russia are two different countries. He called him KGB a few times, and it stuck."

KGB walked in. He was a slim man with a paunch and fat cheeks. The weight didn't suit him, and it was obviously only recently gained.

He had fought in the Bosnian war and gone AWOL when he saw the atrocities the Serbs were committing against the Muslims. Once, while drunk at a bar after he'd helped find evidence in a case I settled for half a million, he told me he'd killed his commander with a knife to the back of the neck. The commander had raped a young Muslim girl and her mother in front of their entire family.

"Anto, thanks for coming."

He sat down next to Olivia without acknowledging her. "What can I do for you?"

Sometimes, I wanted chitchat about the weather, what new cars looked cool, or whom he was dating, but he never provided it. He was to the point and didn't feign any interest in what I was doing. Sometimes, sincere people threw me off guard.

"You know the Pharma Killer case? Someone allegedly poisoning the kids' medicine?"

He nodded.

"A mother of one of the victims thinks this was company negligence and a cover-up, not some psycho lacing the medicine. I've agreed to look into it for them."

He pulled out his phone, along with a stylus for taking notes. "Name?"

"Joel Whiting is the child, twelve years old. The mother bought the cough syrup, Herba-Cough Max, from a grocery store called Greens in their neighborhood. I wanna know how Greens monitors their medicine, whether there're cameras, how sealed and protected the medicine is, stuff like that. I also want you to interview people at Pharma-K. None of the executives. No one from management. Catch some of the secretaries and janitors after work and see if they'll talk to you. There's a secretary named Debbie Ochoa that I really want to talk to. Also, I want the police reports for all three kids that got sick. All the cases were in Salt Lake County."

He nodded. "Anything else?"

"See if you can turn up anything about this company from its past. Any settled lawsuits, claims of negligence, anything like that."

"Okay."

"Oh, and this is Olivia. She'll be working with us on this."

He nodded. "I'll have it to you in a week," he said.

"Sounds good."

As KGB rose, I said to Olivia, "We need to run up to the hospital and see Joel's doctor."

"Why?"

"Because I wanna talk to him before Pharma-K's lawyers do."

---

We were back at the hospital by nine thirty. The hospital sat on the University of Utah campus. I knew Joel's doctor would be in because I had looked him up online. He was a professor of nephrology at the university medical school. His office hours were from ten to noon.

We waited outside his office in the school. The vibe of students running around with their books and the idealistic, hopeful expressions on their faces took me right back. Law school had been like that. Only a few students had approached it in a cutthroat manner. Professors assigned cases out of books in the library, and by the time I'd get there, the pages had been ripped out. But for the most part, there was excitement, and a sense of brotherhood hung in the air. We'd been promised six-figure salaries and a ticket to change the world upon graduation.

The reality was that six-figure salaries existed only for a few. And in exchange, those few worked eighty hours a week for the most miserable lawyers in the country: civil litigators at massive firms.

I always knew I'd make it. I had a vision: the law wasn't a noble profession; it was just a business, no different from any other. No advertisement was too tacky when Marty, Raimi, and I were starting out; no method of getting clients was too lowbrow. One of our most successful ads was a television commercial that featured a beautiful model stripping off her top to reveal the lingerie underneath. Then she said, "I'm waiting for you, but I won't wait forever." And we hit them with the divorce pitch. We ran another ad that showed a good-looking man in a Porsche saying essentially the same thing. The response from horny men and unhappy housewives who had been married too long was overwhelming.

The Bar opened an investigation into complaints that we were actually causing divorces, but the Bar was nothing. It had no real teeth. As long as we didn't steal from our clients and we showed up to all the hearings, a slap on the wrist was all the Bar could hand out. Don't steal, don't lie too much, show up to court—those were the only ethics a lawyer needed.

A man with gray hair and a soft expression approached the office. "Can I help you?"

"Dr. Corwin?" I rose and shook his hand. "Noah Byron. I was wondering if we could talk about Joel Whiting for a minute, Doc."

He looked from me to Olivia and back. "Are you relatives?"

"No," I said with a shy grin, "his lawyer."

As I expected it to, his expression changed. Doctors possessed a built-in animosity toward attorneys. Their insurance companies had convinced them that they were paying fifty thousand dollars a year in medical malpractice insurance because of us, though that wasn't true at all. In Utah, anyone bringing a medical malpractice suit had to first clear a medical panel made up of doctors. If those doctors didn't approve, the potential plaintiff couldn't sue. Doctors looked out for their own, and only truly egregious cases made it through: drunk doctors slipping up during a surgery; a blatantly wrong diagnosis that left the patient dead or disabled. That freed droves of quacks to recommend unnecessary procedures on people, knowing they would never be sued. Still, the insurance companies had pulled a magic trick and convinced doctors it was somehow our fault they were getting milked by their providers.

"I'm afraid I can't discuss his case. You'll have to talk with the office of legal counsel." He turned to leave.

"Doc, I'm just trying to help his mother understand what's going on. She thinks he's going to pass away, and no one's doing anything to help him. I'm just here for her. No malpractice suit, I promise."

He tapped his fingers against his thigh a few times. "Fine. Come in."

His office was neat and sparse. I sat across from him, and Olivia sat next to me. When we were seated, Dr. Corwin said, "What does she have questions about?"

"Are you certain it was cyanide that did this?"

"Is that her asking or you?"

"Both."

"The tests are conclusive. Yes, he had acute cyanide poisoning."

"Can you tell where the cyanide came from? Like, if it was man-made or natural?"

"Natural cyanides are rare. The type found in his blood was inorganic, something commonly used in silver mining, actually."

"Huh. It seems like people would die pretty quick from cyanide. Was this a weaker form?"

"Not really. The amount just wasn't enough to kill, but it did extensive damage. I'm afraid Joel's prognosis isn't good."

I hesitated. "Why isn't he on the transplant list?"

Dr. Corwin's brows drooped and he sighed. "Organs, particularly child organs, are extremely rare. We have to prioritize based on likelihood of survival of the recipient. Joel's kidneys are damaged beyond repair, but his liver is damaged, as well. Within six months, he would need a transplant for that. We also have damage to the heart and lungs that may not even manifest right away. I simply don't know how long he has left. To transplant him now would . . ."

I knew what he was thinking and that he didn't want to say it aloud in front of a lawyer. "Would be a waste of an organ."

"I didn't say that," he quickly added. "It just might take away from someone with a higher chance of survival. It's not an easy decision, but it's one our board had to make."

"But it's not impossible," Olivia said. "I've read there've been cases of people with HIV or other terminal illnesses getting organs. If you really wanted to make it happen, couldn't you?"

"Young lady, there is nothing I'd like more than to give that boy an organ. But to give him one means there's another little boy who won't have one. A little boy who can probably survive and grow old and have children of his own. I'm sorry, but that's just life."

I inhaled deeply. "How long does he have?"

"I don't know. Not long."

I nodded. "Thanks for your time."

I rose to leave, and Olivia followed me out. When we reached the corridor, she shook her head. "He's passing the buck. If one person in this whole process really took a stand and fought for Joel, they'd get him an organ."

"Do you know if a woman is being attacked or beaten, it's actually better to have one person see it than thirty? That's because if there's thirty people that see it, everyone will think someone else will help. If it's only one person, they can't think that way and will likely help. That happened in a rape case in New York. People are set up to pass the buck. I don't blame the doctor."

"Well, that's not depressing or anything." She sighed. "So, what now?"

"I wanna do something really quick. I'll meet you at the car."

———————

I stood outside Joel's room for a second and wondered whether I really should go in there. The case wasn't good, and Walcott was probably the top defense litigation firm in the state. Bob could bury us with money and paperwork and have us tied up in court for the next decade. I touched the doorknob but didn't turn it. Then I looked down both directions of the corridor, turned the knob, and went inside.

Joel was watching television. His mother wasn't there. He smiled when he saw me.

"Hi, Noah."

I stood at the foot of his hospital bed. "Hey." I glanced up at the television. A cartoon was playing. "What you watching?"

"I don't know. I didn't see the name. What're you doin' here?"

"Just came to check up on you. Where's your mom?"

"She went home to get some more clothes." He tried to sit up and grimaced with pain.

"Let me help."

I took him gently under the arms and lifted him higher onto his pillows. He was as light as a blanket. I could feel his bones through his flesh, and the feeling lingered on my hands after I let him go. I pulled up a chair and sat down next to him, staring up at the television.

"I like your name. Noah Byron. It's cool."

I grinned. "Byron's not my given name. I changed it as soon as I turned eighteen."

"Why?"

I considered how to phrase my answer. "My dad wasn't as nice as your dad. So I didn't want to carry his name. The second I turned eighteen, I went to court and changed it."

"Why did you choose Byron?"

"After a poet, Lord Byron. One of my favorites." I smiled at the memory. "I don't think I've read poetry for twenty years."

He thought for a while. "I like it even more since you chose it. It's like you picked your own name. Like you picked who you are."

"Yeah, I guess I did."

He swallowed and reached for a cup of water on the table next to him. I handed it to him.

"Thanks." He drank, then held the cup in his fingers. "My mama said there's a lotta money that we might get if you win your case. I don't care about the money. I just want enough so my mama doesn't have to work anymore. She works at a factory in West Valley for a bad man. She quit so she could be with me, but she'll have to go back. He makes her cry sometimes, but she says she didn't go to college and can't get another job. That's why she says I have to go to college, so I don't have to work for bad men." He took another sip, as though the effort of speaking had dehydrated him. "Can you do that? Can you make it so my mama doesn't have to go back to him?"

I stared at him. "Yeah. Maybe."

He smiled widely. "I knew you were a good man. That's what my mama said about you. That you were a good man God sent here to help us."

I almost chuckled. He completely believed that. Instead, I stood up and looked at the jersey on the wall.

"I never got on the Jumbotron," he said.

"Oh, yeah?"

"Yeah. I really wanted to make silly faces."

"Well, maybe when you get out of here with all your money, you can take your mama there and both be on the Jumbotron."

He smiled. "You really think so?"

"I promise you, buddy, you'll get there."

His entire mood lifted and the smile on his face seemed contagious. "I'll see ya, Joel."

"Noah?" he said as I was walking out.

"Yeah?"

"If you wanted to come over tomorrow, we're gonna have ice cream. My mama's bringing me ice cream from Farr West. It's the best ice cream. Will you come?"

I nodded. "Sure. I'll come."

# 11

The next day, around noon, I was researching cyanide and its effects on the human body when my phone buzzed. I told Jessica to take a message, whoever it was, but she said it was an attorney I knew named Jeppson. I always took Jepp's calls.

"Noah, it's Jepp. How are ya?"

"Good, man. What're you up to?"

"Oh, just finishing up an arbitration. I just wanted to talk to you really quick about something. Bob Walcott called me."

I stopped looking at the computer and leaned back in the chair. "What'd he want?"

"He said you're considering something really stupid and asked if I wouldn't talk some sense into you."

Jepp was an old law school professor of mine, and he'd been one of the first people to refer clients to Byron, Val & Keller. His word was gold with me. I wondered how Bob would know something like that.

"He said that? Those exact words?"

"More or less."

"Why would he care? His firm makes thirty times what we make. He has nothing to be scared of from me."

"Well, he's taking this one kinda personal. He says if you bring a suit and lose, he's going to petition the Bar for sanctions. Maybe even a suspension for bringing a frivolous suit."

"That asshole! I haven't even filed the suit yet, and he's threatening to suspend me?"

"He's got a lotta connections up there, Noah. If he says an attorney should go before a disciplinary council, they'll probably give it to him."

Sometimes, probably just to seem busy, the Bar would look for ways to disbar people. They would conduct stings on attorneys and disbar them the first chance they got. That never happened to the big-name attorneys at the big firms. It was always the little man who got screwed: the working man.

"He's hiding something. Something he's scared I'm going to find."

"Maybe. Or maybe he's old. This is a new, up-and-coming company, and they want him on it personally. Maybe he just doesn't feel like trying cases anymore."

I took a deep breath. Ultimately, I had no control over what Bob did or didn't do.

"Listen," Jepp said, "I'm going to calm him down. Let him know it's just business. I got connections at the Bar, too. I don't think anything will come of it, but I thought I'd relay the message that this is a sensitive one for him."

I couldn't understand why. At $400 million in revenue, Pharma-K wasn't even Walcott's biggest client.

"Well, lemme know if you hear anything else."

"I will. You take care of yourself, Noah."

I stared at the walls for a good five minutes after that, trying to understand why Bob would care so much about this one case. In reality, Pharma-K could pay us off with what would be considered pennies in relation to their revenue and have us sign a nondisclosure agreement so we could never release details about the case or the settlement. This was about more than trying to avoid the bad press from a lawsuit. I was close to something Bob was frightened of.

Raimi poked his head in. "Meeting."

I checked my watch. It was time for our weekly case meeting, where the attorneys gave updates on the major cases the firm was handling. At work meetings, there was a fine line between getting on the same page and just masturbating in a conference room for two hours. Our meetings seemed to cross into the latter territory more often than not.

I hiked over to the conference room, where I found pastries and silver water pitchers with glasses, not paper cups. I sat down at the head of the conference table and leaned back in my seat. Once everyone was seated, the Commandant shouted, "All right, quit your jawin'. Marty, you start."

Marty went into the details of an airline case he was handling. A small plane had gone down over Venezuela while carrying two Americans, both our clients. We suspected there had been a malfunction with the engine, and Marty began discussing the conversation he'd had with our engineers, who would be called as experts in the case.

I zoned out until I spotted Olivia in the corner. She smiled at me, and I grinned. Then I rested my cheek on my palm and listened for the next hour as we went around the table and everyone talked about cases no one else cared about. That was the masturbation part.

Finally, it came to me.

"Noah," Marty said, "what's going on with the Pharma Killer case? We taking it?"

Another attorney, a senior associate with a haircut like an anchorman's, said, "I heard we were handling that. That's awesome."

I stared at him, and he swallowed and looked away.

"Still looking into it. Waiting for a report from KGB."

The anchorman said, "That guy kinda gives me the creeps."

Marty responded, "He's the best investigator I've ever seen. And he's exclusively for partner use. I don't want his time taken up by dog bites and rear-end accidents. He's on our big stuff." He looked at me. "Anything else, Noah?"

I shook my head, and they moved on to the next attorney.

---

The meeting lasted two and a half hours, and I didn't feel like we accomplished much. I rose and was about to leave when the Commandant said, "You have a call with Nyer the Denier in fifteen minutes."

"Shit. Now? I was gonna go to the gym."

"Three-hundred-thousand-dollar case. Get to it and get that money, Mister. Now."

Sometimes, I wondered why the Commandant's name wasn't on the wall. I headed to my office and waited for the call. Roger Nyer was one of the worst insurance adjusters to deal with. He was known as Nyer the Denier because his policy was to outright reject any claim and then negotiate only when he saw the attorneys were serious about pursuing it. This case was a simple car accident where the driver at fault had been drunk, and my client was disabled to the point that she couldn't work. It should've been settled months ago, but instead, Nyer had dragged it out for a year.

Jessica poked her head in. "Noah, Ms. Whiting is on the phone. She said something about waiting for you before they have the ice cream?"

"Oh, right. That. Tell them I can't make it."

"Will do."

I put my feet on the desk and waited for Nyer to call. He never called on time. He had to establish control as quickly as possible, and making a person wait was one of the easiest ways to do that. So I opened Twitter and began flipping through some of the accounts I followed: Ferrari, a few success accounts, and a couple of personal injury ones. It bored me, so I stared out my windows and thought about Tia.

I had known she would move on at some point, but I hadn't expected marriage, even though that was a perfectly logical step for her to take. It'd been three years since the divorce, and she had a right to find happiness.

I wasn't so much bothered that she was having sex with another man—I'd slept with many women since the divorce. Love was something else. Love was the little things. Holding her when her grandmother died and she cried in my arms. Making dinner together. Lying on the grass at the park and watching the clouds. Love was giving our cat a bath that he hated. Sex and dating didn't bother me. What bothered me was that she would do the little things with him now. The little things that, somehow, we had stopped doing. And by the time we realized our relationship was broken, it was too late.

My phone buzzed, and Jessica said Nyer was on the line, twenty-five minutes late.

I answered. "Hey, Roger. How are ya?"

"Fine. I'm calling about—"

"Before you get into it, let's just agree not to jerk each other off, Roger. We're both professionals who have done this too many times to count. I'm going to start high, and you're going to start low. We're gonna haggle for an hour and probably not reach any agreement. Let's save that—I'm not in the mood today. You tell me the highest amount you're willing to offer, and I'll tell you the lowest we're willing to take. Let's see if they overlap at all."

Silence on the other end.

"Roger?"

"I'm here. Who would go first?"

He was smart, this Roger. "I don't know. You have no reason to trust me, and I have no reason to trust you. What if we both say it at the same time?"

"That's childish."

"It would save us both an hour, Roger, and probably an arbitration. Let's just try it."

"Fine. We'll try."

"Okay, on the count of three, we both give the figure. At the same time, okay? On three."

"Fine."

"One . . . two . . . three—blah."

"Two fifty. Shit! You fucker!"

I laughed. "Two fifty it is, Roger. Draft it up."

"You're a damn—"

"I know, I know. Draft it up and send it over with the check. Have a good one."

I hung up. He would never trust me again, of course, but it wasn't as though we'd had a good relationship before.

I rose to get a few other things done around the office, my mood lifted, and my ex effectively fell out of my mind with the thought that I had just made eighty-three thousand dollars.

# 12

That afternoon, I handled a preliminary hearing on a criminal case: a stockbroker accused of market manipulation, which he'd confessed to on video. It was a hopeless case that we would eventually have to deal on, but for now, I wanted to put on a show for the client. Marty was supposed to cover it for me since I was still technically out of the office for the Bethany Chicken trial, but I wanted to be in court again and told him I'd do it myself.

After that was a mediation that went nowhere, then I reviewed some demand letters to insurance companies that my paralegals had drafted. The letters were just summaries of the injuries our clients suffered and the amounts we were asking for. After the demands were received, we would talk to the adjusters, and almost all the cases would end there.

By nightfall, I was actually exhausted from work. That didn't happen often. As I was preparing to leave, I heard women arguing in the hall. Then Rebecca Whiting stormed into my office. She wore jeans and a T-shirt and looked like she'd been crying.

Jessica, trailing behind her, said, "You can't just go in there."

"How could you do that?" she said.

"Excuse me?"

"You told him you would come by the hospital and have ice cream with him."

"I got busy. Did they not tell you?"

"Oh, they told me." She folded her arms. "Mr. Byron, I know how much you're helping us, and I'm very appreciative—more than I could ever tell you. But no one makes a promise to my son and then breaks it. His father used to do that to him all the time, and I would have to be the one to deal with the heartbreak. Joel can't take it now. He doesn't have the strength."

"Rebecca, no offense, but he barely knows me. Why would he care if I came by for ice cream?"

She sighed. "You've never had children, have you?" She turned and stormed out of the office, leaving me staring at Jessica.

---

I was halfway home when I pulled to a stop sign and didn't start moving again. To the east was the hospital, and to the north was my home. I stared up at the lights of the hospital until a horn blared behind me and snapped me out of my thoughts. I started north, then I swerved and went east.

I'd visited a lot of hospitals in my day. In fact, when the law firm first opened, I often hired law clerks to hang out in the cafeterias or walk the halls and listen to conversations. At any hint that someone had been in an accident, our man or woman would strike up a conversation with them. Eventually, the conversation would turn to lawyers, and our name would come up. My clerk would also just happen to slip one of my cards to the injured.

That tactic was strictly prohibited by the Utah State Bar because of some ancient rule that in-person solicitation should be banned because lawyers had some sort of Jedi mind trick that could fool vulnerable people into signing up with us. Third parties working for us were also banned from participating. It was bullshit. The insurance companies had people at hospitals within twenty-four hours to settle big injury suits, knowing full well that the injured people couldn't have talked to a personal injury lawyer by that time. I had a feeling money from the defense side had helped institute that ridiculous rule. I had a moral obligation not to follow it.

For the first year Byron, Val & Keller was in business, we didn't have money for law clerks, so I was the one at the hospitals. I'd been to every damn hospital in the state and ate breakfast, lunch, and dinner at each. I would sit in the cafeteria and listen to the crying. A lot of crying happened in the cafeterias late at night. People would come down with their husbands or wives for a snack, and the pain would just hit them. Sometimes, I could see the change in their faces—the moment when they realized that might be one of the last times they saw the most important person in their life. I heard people's most intimate conversations. When someone thought a loved one wasn't going to make it, they laid all the cards on the table.

I parked and got out. The emergency room was nearly empty as I went down the hall to the adjacent building. The ICU had its own wing, where floor-to-ceiling windows overlooked the city. The lights were beginning to blink on as darkness overtook the city. While I waited for the elevator, I stared out at the buildings. Once, when I was unemployed and sleeping on a cot in a room I shared with three other guys, I'd stared out at the city from a place not unlike this hallway. I'd sworn I would be rich. I smiled, just thinking about it. A kid with nothing—no money, no connections, and no education—had sworn he would be one of the elites. The balls it took to make a promise like that to myself . . .

When I stepped off the elevator, the floor was empty. The nurse behind the desk said that visiting hours were over, and I said I was Joel's lawyer.

"Family only."

"He *is* family," Rebecca said, coming up behind me. "This is my cousin. And he's Joel's lawyer."

The nurse looked from Rebecca to me. "Cousins, huh?"

I signed in, and Rebecca and I walked toward Joel's room. Rebecca didn't say anything, but her face seemed to glow. I still didn't understand why my visit would mean anything to either of them.

She opened the door for me. Joel was playing on a phone. He put it down and grinned when he saw me. He looked puffier than he had the day before.

"Hey," I said. "You got any of that ice cream left?"

"It melted, but we can go down to the cafeteria and get some."

"Joel," his mother said, "they don't like you moving around too much."

He grunted and forced himself up on the bed. "I'm fine. I wanna get outta the room, too."

Rebecca and I helped him up. Joel had one arm around my elbow and the other around his mom's elbow. We started toward a wheelchair pushed up against the wall, but Joel said, "No, I wanna walk."

Rebecca nodded to me, and I got the door as we headed out.

People stared at Joel, and I wondered if he noticed. The cafeteria wasn't far, but it was high up—on the top floor of the building. It sat on the crest of the mountain the hospital had been built on and offered a nearly 360-degree view of the valley. Joel and I sat by the windows while his mom went to get ice cream.

"She's scared," Joel said. "She doesn't have anyone else. Her family isn't in Utah."

"Where are they?"

"Arkansas. That's where I was born. We moved out here for my daddy's job, but then he got sent over there."

I didn't have to ask where "over there" was.

"You miss him a lot, huh?"

"All the time. We was best pals." He swallowed, and I could hear wheezing in his breath. "I remember when those soldiers came to the door. My mama didn't even have to talk to them. She opened the door and started crying. The soldiers held her, and they cried, too. I knew my daddy was dead then." He breathed for a few moments, and I could see the struggle, the difficulty of just doing something everyone else took for granted. "Where's your daddy?"

I shrugged. "I don't know. When I left home, I never called him."

"He's your daddy, though."

"Yeah, well, sometimes I wish we could choose our daddies."

"What'd he do that made you not like him?"

I looked away, a sudden flash of memories I hadn't thought about in a long time filling my mind. I had never discussed my father with anyone but Tia. "He drank a lot. And my mom left us when I was a kid. She fell in love with someone else. I never heard from her again. My dad always said I looked like her. I think he took out his anger at her on me."

Joel was listening intently, though I didn't know if a child of twelve could understand what I'd just told him.

Rebecca had been standing with a group of other people, a set of parents and some kids about Joel's age. She came and sat down. "Brandi and Brandon are here, Joel. Would you like to talk to them?"

He nodded. His mother helped him up and led him over to another table. The two kids sitting there said hi to him. They wore hospital gowns as well. Rebecca came back and pushed a cup of ice cream in front of me as she sat down. I took a spoonful in my mouth and watched Joel. For the first time since I'd met him, he laughed.

"Brandi and Brandon are both here at the Huntsman Cancer Institute. Imagine that? Both your children getting cancer at the same time? They've been here two months, and they come by and visit with Joel. He goes up there sometimes, too."

"Kids his age need friends." I looked at her. "I spoke to his doctor."

"And?"

"And they don't think he can qualify for the transplant list."

"If I had money, I bet he'd qualify. Money to donate to the hospital. The person whose name is on this building wouldn't be denied an organ."

I didn't say anything. We sat in silence, watching as Joel and the other two kids shared games and photos on their phones. The siblings took one photo of Joel making a ridiculous face, then several more with all three of them together.

I pushed the ice cream away from me. I didn't have much of an appetite right now.

"We should get back," Rebecca said. "He can't expend this much energy. It's not good for him."

We went over and helped Joel to his feet. I watched Brandi and Brandon. They were twins, which I hadn't noticed before for some reason, and both looked as healthy as I thought a preteen could look. I saw no hint of what was tearing them apart on the inside.

We led Joel back to his room, and he took out his phone to show me the photo of the face he'd pulled. I smiled. He posted it to his Instagram, and as we helped him back into bed, I heard footsteps in the hallway. Two men appeared at the open door. They looked surprised to see me.

I recognized one of them—a man named Cole Harding, an attorney with Walcott.

I stepped between them and Joel. "You gotta be shitting me," I said.

"No letter of representation's been sent. You're not officially his attorney yet," Cole said. "We can interview him if we want."

"Interview?"

"Noah, he is not your client yet. Our firm is perfectly within our rights to interview someone who may—"

"Get the hell outta this room. And if you come back, I'll file a TRO to make sure you can't even come into this hospital again. I don't think any judge is going to be too happy that you tried to take advantage of a child who's already represented."

The two men looked at each other, then went away.

"What was that about?" Rebecca asked.

"That was about being careful. Which we'll have to do from now on. They wanted to try to catch Joel in a position where he might say something that would hurt any future lawsuit."

"Like what?"

"Like something that might indicate he was sick before he took their medication or that he has a genetic predisposition—something like that."

"But he doesn't. He got sick after he took the medicine."

"Rebecca, the law has nothing to do with what actually happened. It's about what a jury hears. That's all. They want to make you guys look bad." I glanced toward the door. "They won't be back, though. I'll make sure." I turned to Joel. He looked exhausted just from the effort of going up to the cafeteria for a few minutes. "I'll keep in touch, Joel. My investigator, a man named Anto, is going to come interview you soon. Don't talk to anyone else unless you have my say-so, okay?"

"Okay. Thanks for coming here."

"You're welcome. I'll see ya soon."

I nodded to Rebecca and headed out of the room. When I was out in the hall, I called Jessica's cell phone. Not many legal secretaries made eighty thousand a year, but I wanted access at all hours in exchange for that money. Still, I never abused the privilege and had used it only a few times.

"Hi," she said. "What's up?"

I could hear the pen click in her hand. "Joel Whiting. I'm taking the case. Send a letter to Walcott, informing them I'm Joel's lawyer, and tell them to keep the hell away from him. Send letters to Pharma-K's insurance and the Attorney General's office, too."

"AG? What for?"

"Walcott's got connections everywhere, and Pharma-K brought hundreds of jobs to this state. The government isn't gonna like that we're filing suit. I'll bet you lunch the AG's office gets involved and stands next to Walcott during a press conference. Send them a letter now, telling them to keep away from Joel, too."

"Anything else?"

"Get a rep agreement to Rebecca Whiting." I paused. "And, um, get our videographer ready. We need to record Joel's statement in case he's not . . . around for the trial."

"Okay. And Noah? You're doing the right thing for that family."

"Yeah, well, not if I get my butt kicked."

# 13

KGB updated me on the investigation a couple of days after I'd had ice cream at the hospital. He always said a job would take longer than it really would, then surprised us with how quickly he could get it done.

I read the police reports while he sat in my office, wearing earbuds, listening to some new age music. He closed his eyes as though he were meditating.

The police reports were sparse. They included interviews with people at the pharmacies and grocery stores where the tainted medicine had been found, as well as interviews with the victims and the victims' families. None of that actually helped determine what had happened. One report stated that an officer had spilled some of the tainted cough medicine on his fingers and felt ill afterward, though he'd survived after being sick for a few days.

The reports ended with a sentence stating that the investigation was ongoing. What they meant was they had nothing. The investigators speculated that the poisoner might have been a driver who delivered to the three stores. They didn't even consider that it could've been someone at the plant that had made the medicine to begin with. I was looking at shoddy police work all around. The FBI had been notified and come in to complete their own investigation, but those reports weren't available yet. I hoped they were more thorough than what I was looking at.

"Is it good?" KGB said loudly.

"No. These cops didn't know what they were doing. They didn't even connect the three poisonings until Joel's nurse had his cough medicine tested. They interviewed a couple of people at Pharma-K, but just the delivery drivers. No one on the floor of the plant."

"Hmm."

"Damn right, 'hmm.'" I picked up the phone and dialed the Salt Lake County Sheriff's Office. When I asked for Detective Cynthia Lyne, I was transferred, and she said hello.

"Hi, Detective. My name is Noah Byron, and I'm an attorney for one of the families in the Pharma Killer case. I was wondering if I could just speak to you for a minute."

She hesitated. "Sure."

"Great. Well, first, it doesn't look like there's any interviews with any of the supervisors or executives at Pharma-K. Did you interview them?"

"We interviewed one vice president, but he didn't have anything relevant to add."

"And you didn't include that report in the official case file?"

"Like I said, it wasn't relevant. But it should be in a supplemental report somewhere."

"What about any of the workers on the floor of the plant? The medicine is actually made there. Did you visit the plant?"

"Yes, we interviewed—I believe—three people over there."

"But no foremen or supervisors?"

"No. They showed us their operations. We didn't think the poison could've come from their end."

"Why not?"

"They've got strict protocols in place. They don't allow interaction between employees and the medicine until the inspection just before the lid is put on, and only one man at a time does the inspection."

I thought for a second. "Who gave you the tour?"

"One of the vice presidents and their lawyer."

Their lawyer. Walcott had been involved from early on. Again, that could just mean they were frightened about the potential for a lawsuit, or it could mean something else.

"Did anybody at the plant have criminal records? Anyone you looked into?"

"A few people, but nothing serious. Some DUIs and things like that." She paused. "This is an ongoing investigation, Counselor. I'm strictly speaking to you out of courtesy for those families. I won't reveal anything that I wouldn't consider making public."

"I understand. Did you ask Pharma-K if this had ever happened before?"

"Yes, and it never has. They're a pretty new company. Haven't really had time yet to screw up."

"The medicine my client took came from Greens Groceries. There's cameras there, and the shelf is right next to the cashiers. Did you review the video?"

She hesitated, and I knew she hadn't obtained the video. "I think I've said all I'm going to say for now."

"Okay, well, I appreciate your time, Detective." I hung up. "Lazy all around, Anto."

KGB looked at me and smiled.

"They didn't even review the video at the grocery store."

He shrugged. "Maybe they have it and are getting to it?"

"Yeah, maybe. So, did you find Debbie Ochoa?"

"No. She was fired from the company after the poisoning. She doesn't live in the state anymore."

"She doesn't live in the state? This happened like three weeks ago."

He nodded. "She moved. Tried calling. Phone is disconnected."

"Find her, Anto. I don't care how long it takes."

"Will do."

"Did you interview anyone at Pharma-K?"

He shook his head. "They would not talk. They seem scared. One man say they would be fired."

"It's probably more than that. I bet Walcott held a meeting with all the employees and made them sign gag orders so they couldn't speak to anyone without a court order. We'll have to do it in the depositions, if it gets that far."

"You do not think it will?"

I wasn't sure. Almost nothing about this case so far had gone the way I expected. Still, I went with what my experience said.

"I think they'll throw enough money at us to make us go away. Olivia said this case was on TV. Did either of the other families have lawyers?"

"One, but he drop the case."

"Why?"

"I talk to him. He say too much money to fight."

I swallowed and leaned back in my seat. A ball of anxiety grew in the pit of my stomach. The lawyer was probably right: liability wasn't at all clear, and this case was going to take a lot of money to investigate.

"You want I stop?" Anto said.

I watched him a second: the round, pale face and the crystal-blue eyes that took me in without judgment. "No. Keep digging. There's something there they don't want us to find."

# 14

KGB continued the investigation, and within a few weeks, we had more than the police had in their file. We had company histories that even Pharma-K's stockholders didn't have. And we had background checks on every employee at the plant.

Olivia sat across from me in my office. We'd ordered in Chinese for lunch, and empty cartons littered my desk as the two of us pored over the documents KGB had collected. Olivia had a look of concentration on her face like a laser beam. It seemed like she wasn't even blinking as she read. I was the opposite: details bored me, and I liked to focus on the big picture. I was suddenly glad she was here, and not working some bankruptcy for Raimi.

"Anything?" I finally said, leaning back in the seat and rubbing my eyes.

"Take a look at this," she said, pulling out a page from a thick stack of papers. "It's a statement from one of the floor workers at the plant. He quit, got another job, and so I don't think he was scared to write this."

I looked at the statement. It said that he and his coworkers had been ordered by higher-ups at Pharma-K not to discuss this case with anyone, and if they knew any details about it, to immediately see their supervisor to determine what to do.

"Not exactly the actions of a company with nothing to hide, is it?" she said.

I tossed the statement on the desk. "No, it's not."

"How many cases like this have you done before?"

"Depends what you mean. I've sued a lot of companies, but never one that made such a concerted effort to hide everything."

She took a sip from a bottle of water and stared at the sunlight shining through it when she placed it back on the desk. "My mom, back when I was young, needed to be hospitalized in a mental health care center. She was in there for, like, thirty days or something. The insurance company was supposed to cover it. We got a letter saying they weren't because the hospitalization wasn't medically necessary. I called them every day, I emailed them, I called the police and the FBI—I was like fifteen then, so I didn't know any better. I did everything I could, but they would only send us letters that they weren't going to pay. No explanation, no one to talk to. They knew we were too weak to fight them on it and they took advantage of that."

"What'd you do?"

"I couldn't do anything. So I started learning how to knit and make jewelry at home that I could sell. The only asset my mom had was that house and I didn't want the hospital to take it. It took me four years of monthly payments to pay them off. That's what this is. I know it. It just feels the same, the way the company's responding."

"Feeling's got nothing to do with it; we gotta convince a jury. And that takes witnesses. Make a note to subpoena that guy."

Olivia and I drafted and sent a letter to Walcott, stating that we intended to file a claim. Two days later, his secretary called Jessica to set up a negotiation. Usually, we just spoke over the phone, but on large cases, the negotiation became a big deal. The plaintiffs would bring all their lawyers, and the defense would bring all their. Then we would meet on neutral ground. We would hash it out all day and see if we could reach a number both sides could live with. I'd once rented a restaurant that sat on the roof of a building in downtown Salt Lake, and we'd spent three days there, negotiating a medical malpractice case where the doctor, high on heroin, had inserted the wrong valve during a heart repair.

The meeting with Walcott was set, and I rented the same restaurant. Because they couldn't serve other customers while we were there, the price tag was steep but worth it. We would have seclusion, food, and drink, and Walcott would be impressed that I'd sprung for it. People tended to think others were serious about something if they spent more money on it.

We headed up to the Gold Lion's Restaurant and Grill. This time, I brought my entire team. There was no jury to be the underdog in front of. In negotiation, I wanted to be intimidating.

A long conference table had been set up in the middle of the restaurant. The owner, a man named Jerry, said hello, and I ordered wine. Walcott didn't drink during work hours, but I thought the mood might strike him. I could get a lot more out of him if he was drunk.

Our firm's attorneys took our places, and within minutes, Walcott's people began to file in, lawyers all around. We had brought twelve, and they had thirteen. I texted the Commandant to get two more lawyers there immediately.

I sat in the middle of the conference table, and Bob sat across from me. Everyone exchanged pleasantries—everyone except me and Bob. We both sat quietly and only occasionally made eye contact. We waited a solid ten minutes until the conversations died down. My two additional lawyers, two people from the family law section headed by Marty, had arrived. Marty sat on one side of me, and Raimi sat on the other.

Olivia was farther down, but I could see her. One of the men on the other side of the table was flirting with her.

"Shall we get started?" Bob asked.

"Certainly."

Negotiations on a PI case at such an early stage were dangerous. Until we officially filed the complaint, the document initiating a lawsuit, we weren't entitled to the evidence in the case. No depositions had been conducted, and no interrogatories—long legal questionnaires covering everything a lawyer could think to include—had been sent. But it worked in reverse, too: Bob didn't know how much I knew. Both sides went into the first negotiation blind. It was a terrible way to settle cases, but I was willing to take less because I didn't know the scope of the case, and the defense was willing to offer more because they didn't know what I had.

"What do you want, Noah?"

"What would you like to give me, Bob?"

We sat silently again, the lawyers around us not saying anything, for a long time. Finally, Raimi pulled out his figures.

"The current medical costs for our client," he said, "are one hundred seventy thousand and forty-two cents. This is purely special damages. General damages are estimated at three hundred and fifty thousand for pain, suffering, and emotional distress. Should the child die in the next three months, as his physicians predict, the suit would transfer to a wrongful death claim for the mother. We would at that point ask for two million, one hundred seventy-one thousand, and sixty-three cents."

"Sixty-three cents, huh?" Bob said with a smirk.

"You know Raimi," I said. "You ever know him to throw in numbers that haven't been through at least a dozen calculations?"

Bob raised his eyebrows. "So you want half a million dollars now to avoid a two-million-dollar lawsuit if the boy dies. Sounds like extortion to me, Noah."

I smiled. "I don't want half a million dollars. Those numbers Raimi gave you, triple them. That's how much I'm asking for. When I get that boy on the stand, no jury in the world is going to say no to me."

"I think you overestimate how much weight juries give to the testimony of plaintiffs. After we're through painting his mother as a gold digger looking for a quick payday, you'd be lucky to get his medicals paid for. And that's even if you somehow proved negligence on the part of my client, which I don't think you can."

I leaned back in my seat. I looked over the faces of the lawyers seated across from me. These were the same lawyers who had denied me jobs, looked down on me because I hadn't gone to the right schools, and felt that they were above me and above anybody who wasn't like them.

"I don't need to win this case to ruin your client. I'll scream negligent poisoning to the media every chance I get. Who is possibly going to buy a Pharma-K-brand medicine when there's perfectly good alternatives from companies that haven't been accused of poisoning their customers? Doesn't matter whether it's true or not. People just won't risk buying your brand."

Bob looked over at Darren Rucker. The two exchanged glances but didn't say anything.

"What's your final number?" Bob asked.

"Three point five million is what I would normally ask for. But, because it's early in the case, I'll ask for half that. Consider also, Bob, that the other two kids who got sick from your client's medicine haven't approached our firm yet. When we get some media attention, maybe they'd like to join suit."

Bob exhaled through his nose and looked to Darren. "Give us a moment."

"Of course."

The two of them, along with three others from their side of the table, rose and went into a separate room of the restaurant.

Raimi leaned over and said, "That's too much. They won't pay."

"They'll pay."

"A child from a poor family doesn't have earning capacity, Noah. They're worth the least of any demographic. They're invisible. Bob won't pay, and we'll have to litigate."

"He'll pay. Watch."

A few people ordered drinks and appetizers. I rose from the table and wandered around. I found a balcony in a small room in the back and went outside. The sky was overcast, and a breeze was blowing. Rain wouldn't be far behind. I stared out over the city I had promised myself I would conquer. It was growing so fast that if I didn't stop to look at it sometimes, I wouldn't recognize it the next time I did.

"Noah," Olivia said as she came up behind me, "they're back."

"Thanks."

"You okay?" she said, stepping out onto the balcony.

"Yeah, fine. I was just thinking about something from a long time ago."

"What?"

"It's embarrassing."

"Tell me."

I turned toward her. "When I first moved to this city, I swore to myself I would own it one day. That I'd be a big shot. I was just thinking about what I was like then. So hungry. I would've stepped over corpses to get what I wanted. I don't know if I'm like that anymore. You think the things we want just kind of fade over time?"

"I don't know. I know we have something inside us that doesn't change. Not ever. Maybe you thought getting money and power was that thing for you, but you were wrong?"

"Did you grow up very poor?"

"Yeah, but I didn't really know anything else so it never bothered me much."

"I grew up so poor I'd be lucky most days to eat one meal. Sometimes I would have to go for two or three days without food. My shoes had so many holes in them it would've been just as easy to go barefoot.

That kind of poverty . . . you know, people tell you when you get rich and you come from that, that it was necessary. That you wouldn't appreciate what you have if you didn't suffer first. It's not true. Poverty cuts deep, and I don't know if the pain ever leaves."

She placed her hand on my shoulder. I straightened up and said, "Let's not keep his highness waiting."

---

I took my place at the table. Bob took his and straightened his tie. He looked at me and smiled before pouring himself a cup of water and taking a drink. He set the cup down.

"That's high," Bob said. "But my client doesn't want to drag this out, and they certainly would like to help the family of anyone hurt by their product. One million flat. Payable today with a gag order barring any discussion in any public forum."

Raimi wrote a note on the napkin in front of him that said, "Take it!"

"I'll discuss it with my client tonight. You'll have our answer in the morning."

Bob rose and didn't shake my hand. Some of the other lawyers followed suit, but some of them said good-bye. The one flirting with Olivia asked for her number, and she gave it to him. I turned away. Marty was right there, with a smile on his face.

"I did not think they would offer that."

I shrugged. "They don't want this in the news anymore."

Marty, the smile still on his face, said, "I think it's time to ditch Penny and go out and get smashed with the boys. What do you two say?"

I watched Olivia for a moment. "Lemme go to the hospital and tell them to take the offer first."

---

As I drove to the hospital, I thought about how I could've just texted Rebecca and told Bob right then whether we would accept the offer or not. But I wanted him to stew for the night. Let him try to soothe the nerves of Pharma-K and assure them that this would all be a memory soon. I wanted at least one night where I had the upper hand.

Rebecca was in the ICU hallway, staring into the room. She was crying.

"What's wrong?" I said.

"He just . . . he just . . ."

She couldn't speak. She threw her arms around me and sobbed.

My heart dropped. I looked into the room and saw several doctors and nurses working on Joel.

"He just stopped breathing," she blurted through tears.

We stood in the hallway for a while, until I could get her over to some chairs and sit her down. I then went to the nurses' station and asked them what was going on. The nurse simply said they were doing everything they could.

The door flew open, and they wheeled Joel out. Rebecca screamed. I could see him lying on the bed, but he didn't look the way he had the last time I'd seen him. He was as white as a sheet of paper and sweating so profusely, it had soaked the pillow and his hospital gown. They wheeled him away, and Rebecca ran after him. A nurse gently took her arms and prevented her from following the crew. Joel was wheeled around the corner, then he was gone.

# 15

I sat in one of the chairs next to Rebecca in the waiting room. Olivia texted me and asked if they had accepted the offer. I told her what had happened and that I wouldn't be bringing it up right now. Within twenty minutes, Olivia walked through the doors. She wore workout clothes and looked like she'd come from the gym. She sat down next to us without a word.

None of us spoke. Rebecca was biting her fingernails so obsessively that I thought her fingers might bleed. I gently took her hand and held it. We sat like that for a long time. A television was playing in the corner with the sound turned low; some game show was on. We were the only ones there. Eventually, Olivia rose and turned it off.

"Do you have anyone I should call?" I said. "Any family you want out here?"

She shook her head. "My parents are both passed, and I only had one sibling, a brother. I don't know where he is. New York, I think. We never talk. I have an aunt. But she's got enough problems without worrying about me."

"What about Joel's grandparents from his dad's side?"

"They're drunks somewhere down south. Last I heard they were living in a trailer park in Florida. They couldn't care less about Joel. They barely cared about his father."

"What about Tia?"

"I don't want to bother her with this. She's got a new fiancé and all and a life to start." She looked up at me. "Sorry."

"It's true. Don't apologize."

"Do you miss her?"

I wanted to look at Olivia, but resisted the urge. "Whatever we had is gone," I said. "Divorce does that. So you don't want me to call anybody?"

She breathed out through her nose. "There's no one to call. It's just me and him."

A man in blue scrubs came in. He sat down and said, "He's stable."

"Oh!" Rebecca squealed, the tears coming again.

"We're going to recommend increasing his dialysis. Dr. Corwin is on his way down here and will explain everything. There's some medication we can try, as well, that we haven't used yet."

"Will it happen again?"

The doctor was silent for a second. "I don't know."

He said that Rebecca could see Joel, but that he was resting. She followed him back, leaving me and Olivia in the waiting room.

"You didn't have to come," I said.

"I wanted to."

"No hot date tonight with that attorney from Walcott?"

She grinned. "You noticed that, huh? He did call. We were supposed to have dinner."

"There's no reason for both of us to be here. You're young—you should be out on dates. Go have fun. I have it covered."

"Actually, I feel like some cafeteria food, if you want to join me."

"You sure? This isn't exactly where I would want to spend a Friday night if I were you."

"I'm sure."

The cafeteria was nearly empty. The food looked a little hammered, as it was the end of the day, but the enchiladas appeared edible. I wasn't hungry, but I didn't feel like just sitting there, either, so I got the enchiladas and a tea. Olivia got a cookie and chocolate milk. We sat at a table by the windows and watched the crowds heading out on the town.

"I thought that was brave," she said. "How you asked for so much money. All the clerks were talking about it after."

"There's nothing brave about it. It's just greed."

"I don't think that's true."

"I don't think I am who you think I am, Olivia."

She thought for a moment. "You're the kind of guy who's at a hospital on a Friday night because you know your client doesn't have anyone else to be here with him." She bit into her cookie and stared out the windows. After a while, she sighed and looked around. "You never get used to the smell of the hospital. It's this weird, kind of antiseptic smell. I've been in so many, I thought I wouldn't notice it anymore."

"I used to have to go with my dad all the time. He would get drunk and fall down the stairs or hit his head somewhere and cut it open."

"I didn't know my dad. They never talked again after they hooked up after a dance."

"Just one dance?"

"Just one. My mom was kind of a slut in the eighties."

I grinned. "How old are you?"

"Twenty-nine. You?"

"Thirty-six."

"Whoa."

"That old, really?"

"No," she said. "It's not that. You're just so young to be so successful."

"Although I bet I was the type of lawyer your torts professor warned you about. The kind that gives us a bad name and that you should never be like no matter how much you're starving."

"How'd you know?"

"Because they told me that, too. It made me want to be that lawyer more. I didn't intend to slave away in a law library and just be content that I was part of some grand profession. I wanted to be rich. I thought law was a good way to do that. But there were a million different ways I could've done it without law school."

"Seems to have worked out for you."

"A nearly forty-year-old guy, once divorced, whose best friends, who are also his business partners, are slowly drifting away from him, and his ex-wife is marrying his polar opposite?"

"No, someone who has the admiration of everyone working for him. You should hear the associates and clerks talk about you. How awesome you are in court, how insurance defense lawyers are scared of you, how much money you get for our clients."

"Yeah," I said, then took a bite of the enchilada. "There is that." The enchilada was cold and rubbery. "This reminds me of elementary school food."

"No, elementary school food was better."

"I know a place. Let's go check in with Rebecca and go there."

"Sure, why not. I have nothing planned but watching *Vampire Diaries* tonight."

———

We tried to check on Joel, but they wouldn't let us into the room. I texted Rebecca that I was leaving.

I knew of a restaurant by the University of Utah. It primarily made its money as a bar catering to students, but a few people knew about the great food. We parked in the lot behind the pharmacy next door and hiked up a hill to get to the joint.

Inside was dark, but not smoky like it had been a decade ago. Smoking in public places had been banned in Utah, with an exception carved out for a few bars that functioned only as bars and not as restaurants. We sat at a table in the center.

"Can I order for you?" I said.

"Sure."

"Two of Dom's pizzas," I said to the waitress. "And two beers."

"Actually, I don't drink. Just a Coke, please," she said to the waitress.

The drinks came, and we took a few sips. Olivia seemed distracted. Her eyes would search the restaurant, then rest somewhere, and she would stare at that spot for a long time.

"What are you thinking about?" I finally asked.

"Just my mom. Sometimes I get home and she's okay, and sometimes, she's having an episode. I never know which it will be."

"Can't be easy for either of you."

"It has its moments. I think it's just hard because I still remember what she was like before the episodes started getting worse. Until I was ten, she was just like any other mom. Then the episodes started happening and I knew something was wrong. The medication helps, though. An antipsychotic that's kind of new. Without it I never would've been able to leave her long enough to go to law school. But it kind of levels her out. She used to paint, and once she started the medication, she couldn't do it anymore. She had a little studio and just completely abandoned it."

"I've heard of things like that. I had a friend I used to share an apartment with. Really creative guy. There'd always be drawings of these magnificent buildings up on the walls. Stuff I've never seen before or since. He became an architect, but needed bipolar medication. Once he started the medication, he couldn't work. Couldn't come up with anything. He had to get off the medication so he wouldn't lose his job."

"That's wild. Is he doing okay?"

"No," I said. "He punched his boss in the face during a manic episode and got fired."

She snorted, then immediately covered her mouth. "I'm sorry. I know that's not funny."

"No, it's fine. He opened his own office, and he's good now. Still not taking his meds, though."

She sipped her drink. "What about you? Have you been to therapy?"

I grinned, then guzzled half my glass. "That's a little personal for a first date, isn't it?"

"I didn't know we were on a date."

"We're not. Forget I said that. I don't want to get sued."

"I think I'd hire Bob Walcott as my lawyer. He'd get a kick out of suing you."

"Yeah, he definitely would."

"What happened to his eye?"

"I think he's faking it."

"No!"

I nodded, taking another drink. "That's the rumor. He fakes it to intimidate everyone. But all the plaintiffs' lawyers think he's faking it, so I don't know who he thinks he's fooling. Maybe you do something long enough, and you can't stop."

She shook her head. "Weird. What's with you two, by the way? It seems personal."

"When I first started, he took advantage of my naivety and screwed my client. I've never forgiven him. We've worked together a few times since then, but I usually let Marty or Raimi handle it."

That reminded me that I had told my partners I would meet them. I took out my phone and saw I had two texts from Marty, asking where I was. I replied that I would be late and to get started without me.

"If you need to go, it's cool."

"No, it's fine. I like it here. Reminds me of being in college. You went to BYU, didn't you? What'd you major in?"

"You didn't read my resume?"

"Honestly, I only looked at your extracurriculars."

"Oh, yeah? You were impressed by my violin playing and chess?"

"Something like that."

"I majored in math."

"Seriously? Why would you possibly become a lawyer if you could be a mathematician?"

"I don't know. Same as everyone else, I guess. Just want to help people."

"There're better ways to help people. You could work for a non-profit or something."

"Nonprofits need lawyers, too. Why do you hate the profession so much?"

"I don't hate it," I said, holding up a finger, "I don't hate it." I leaned back in my chair. The alcohol was warming my stomach and loosening my muscles. "I just think it's a sham. It's not what anybody thinks it is, and there's a new law school popping up every day. People who don't know what else to do with their lives become lawyers, and the market shrinks for everybody. It's a race to the bottom. Within a few decades, lawyers will be charging so little, you won't be able to survive on it. The day of even the middle-class trial lawyers is gone."

"That's depressing, considering I'm just barely starting out."

"Don't do it."

"Do what?"

"Become a lawyer. Find something else that you love and do that. The law is swimming with sharks because we've eaten all the fish. Don't do it."

"Wow. Didn't think I'd hear that from my boss."

I shrugged, finished my beer, and ordered another.

# 16

Olivia and I ate and drank well into the night. She had a casualness that was pleasant to be around. She was one of those people who could make strangers feel as if they'd known her their entire lives.

We talked about my life working as a ranch hand in Arizona after high school and about what had led me to law school. It was really just a billboard, one I think everyone else hated. A lawyer—I don't even remember his name now—was sitting on the hood of his Ferrari and saying, "Accident? You wanna be rich? Call me today." I didn't even register the "accident" or the "call me today" portions. All I saw was a giant billboard that said, "You wanna be *rich?*"

At the time, I had six dollars in my checking account, and my job, which was seasonal, was ending in two weeks. The billboard spoke to me more than almost anything ever had. I quickly finished my bachelor's degree in a night program while I waited tables during the day, and then I applied to six law schools. University of Kansas was the only one that accepted me, and I was approved for student loans to cover tuition. I loaded up on credits each semester and took summer classes, too—as many as I could. I finished law school in two years rather than three, then clerked for a nearby solo practitioner who focused on personal injury. I analyzed the markets for personal injury law and found that Utah, despite its two law schools pumping out graduates, had a low number of personal injury lawyers per capita. Only North and South Dakota had lower numbers, but I sure as hell wasn't moving to either of those. I packed up one gym bag and took the Bar in Utah.

Olivia seemed amazed by the fact that someone could just pick up and move their entire life at the drop of a hat. She'd never lived anywhere except the house she had been born in and one summer in California.

Her experience of law school was a lot different than mine, too: she aced every class, was on the staff of every prestigious journal, and didn't even seem to need to study. She said she would just glance at the assigned reading and know what the professors were looking for. For me, law school consisted of two years of pain and frustration. For her, it was a time to relax and get to know her fellow students.

I didn't remember I was supposed to meet Marty and Raimi until I was home in bed.

---

I woke up the next morning and didn't have a hangover. I even went for a quick jog before coming home to make coffee and have a croissant. When enough time had passed, I called Rebecca.

"How is he?" I asked.

"He's awake now. We're just watching television. They think he can go back to ICU this afternoon."

"Rebecca, I need to talk to you about something. An offer's been made on Joel's case."

"Already?"

"Yeah, it's customary to negotiate at the outset on something like this, even though both sides don't have all the information yet. They offered one million. Our firm would get a third of that, and the rest would go to you. You probably wouldn't ever have to work again if you were careful with the money."

"And they're going to come out publicly and say what happened?"

"No, the opposite. They'll draft a gag order for a judge to sign. It'll state that you can't ever talk about the case to anyone in public. If the terms of the deal ever got out, they could sue you."

"They won't even apologize? They're going to get away with this?"

"We don't know for sure how much they're liable for this. There could very well be some maniac out there poisoning children's medicine. It's weird that it's only one medicine and only in one geographic location and that there haven't been any additional cases, but that doesn't preclude the possibility that this was one person who tampered with a few bottles after the cough syrup was already in stores. Pharma-K is offering this money to get this case out of the news and move on. The more people hear about it, the fewer will buy their cough medicine and other products."

Silence a moment.

"I don't know what to do," she said. "I don't care about the money. I don't want this to happen to anyone else's child. And I want to know why my son is dying. You can't imagine how important that is. But I'll do whatever you say. I trust you. If you say to take it, I'll take it."

I leaned against my kitchen counter. I could tell her to take it, and our firm would have over three hundred thirty-three thousand in the bank by the end of the week. I could tell her not to take it, and we might spend five times that litigating this thing.

The first thought that entered my mind was of Joel being wheeled around that corner. He'd looked so out of it, as if he could go at any second. Rebecca was right: if Pharma-K had anything to do with this, they were getting away with it. No one would ever find out what happened, and it might happen again to someone else. But that wasn't my problem, was it? I was their lawyer, not their family counselor.

I opened my mouth to tell her to take it, but then I stopped. I kept playing that scene over and over again: Joel being rushed around a corner, doctors working frantically to save his life.

"Don't take it," I said. "We can ask for ten times that from a jury, and we might get it if we can show fault on the company's part. Even if it's just that they didn't tamperproof the medicine well enough."

"Okay, I won't take it. So what happens now?"

I sighed. "Now we go to war."

# 17

The first step in litigation was interrogatories—long questionnaires sent between the parties to gather as much information as possible. I set up a command center in the first conference room and recruited Olivia, two associates, and a paralegal to do nothing but work on Joel's case. The first morning, I went through all the types of questions I wanted asked. We covered every relevant question and all the irrelevant ones. Are you married? How long? Do you have kids? Do you have a dog? What's your religion? How do you feel about Pharma-K? How many years have you lived in this state? What did you do when you heard about the injuries to the three children?

We drafted well into the evening. I left and went home to sleep, but sleep didn't come right away. I stayed up most of the night staring at the ceiling. Joel's case was going to be a true battle. When I'd called Bob to tell him we wouldn't take the deal, he started banging his phone against his desk.

He threw every cuss word he could think of at me before he screamed, "He's fucking invisible!"

I didn't even respond. I just hung up. I didn't know why I thought this case had such a high valuation, but something in Pharma-K's behavior told me I had to know what they were hiding. The trick was not bankrupting the firm in the process. If costs weren't controlled—with experts, depositions, briefs, pulling resources away from other cases, and the opportunity cost of turning other cases down to work on this—we could easily spend a million in a year. If the case dragged on for a few years, our firm would be out of money.

When I arrived at the office the next morning, Olivia was still in the conference room, with the paralegal, drafting away. Only the lawyers had gone home. Raimi came up behind me, and Marty came in front.

"Are you crazy?" Marty said. "They offered seven figures."

"We can't take it."

"Why?"

"Because they're hiding something."

"So what? Everybody's hiding something. They offered seven figures."

Raimi said, "It was far in excess of the value of this case, Noah. You need to advise the client to take it."

"They offered seven figures!"

"Guys," I said, "when have I ever screwed us? Hmm? Can you think of one time I took a big case and it didn't pan out? We will get more for this case."

"How much more?"

"I'm going to ask for ten million."

Marty laughed. "You're outta your mind. Are you on drugs? Is that what this is?"

"They will pay us. We just need to push them a little bit."

"How much?"

"I don't know—a little bit."

Raimi shook his head. "They offered at least twice what this case is worth to settle it. If they perceive that we think we can keep getting more by pushing this along, they'll feel it's better to risk a trial."

"And we'll settle before that point. But for now, I think we can get a lot more."

I brushed past the two of them and went to my office. I shut the door behind me and sat at the desk. I unplugged my office phone, then turned to the windows and looked down at the streets. Raimi was right: they had offered far more than the case was worth. Even if they had offered to pick up the medical bills, it would've been a gift. As far as anyone knew, Pharma-K had nothing to do with the poisoning. Doubt still lingered, though. If I could plant that doubt in a jury's mind, they might side with us. And in a civil case, I didn't need every juror, just a simple majority of them.

The worst thing that could happen to this case, of course, was if the police made an arrest. If some crazy hillbilly with no connection to Pharma-K was the one poisoning the medicine, we were sunk. The company wouldn't even pick up the medical bills at that point, and Rebecca Whiting would be out her million dollars. We needed to speed this litigation along before that could happen.

I plugged my phone back in and dialed Jessica.

"Yeah?" she said.

"Get Luke to draft the complaint for the Whiting case. Tell him I'd like it filed within twenty-four hours. Once it's filed, I want the soonest court date we can get."

"Gotcha. Which court?"

I hadn't even thought about venue. Wherever we filed the lawsuit was going to have a big impact on the outcome. Federal courts had jurors who were typically more educated and better informed, but that might not be a bonus in this case. Maybe we wanted the average Joe Schmoe who would imagine himself in the position of Rebecca Whiting.

"I want it in state court," I said.

"Okay. We'll get it done."

"Thanks."

I left my office and went back to the conference room. The two attorneys still weren't there, and only the paralegals and Olivia were working.

"Sally," I shouted down the hall.

"What?" came a reply from somewhere in the guts of the office.

"Get me two more of Raimi's guys."

"Okay. Give me an hour."

One thing about the Commandant: she never questioned orders. I stepped inside the conference room and shut the door.

# 18

On a big case, interrogatories could take months. In this case, they took two weeks. We received vague answers on the 112 of them that we sent. In turn, on the two we'd received for Rebecca and Joel, we also gave vague answers.

Meanwhile, KGB scored the surveillance video from Greens. On the date Rebecca bought her medication, it showed her picking up the medicine, paying for it, and leaving. I paid Anto to watch the entire video for that day and the day before. No one had tampered with the medicine the day Rebecca bought it, or the day before.

The first court date had been set. We placed the case at the West Jordan District Court, and a judge named Gills had been assigned.

I had been in front of Nathan Gills only once. I'd tried a dog-bite case to the bench—meaning the judge, not a jury, was the decider— and lost. I'd thought it wasn't a terrible case, but Gills had disagreed. Though, in fairness, we should have lost that case because liability wasn't clear.

The main thing I remembered about him was his proclivity for swearing while on the record. I initially thought I misheard him, but then he'd kept doing it. I'd asked the bailiffs about it afterward, and they had said that was how he was.

The morning of court, I met with Olivia. Though we had four other actual attorneys on the case, I had made her my lead on Joel's case. She was passionate about it in a way the other four weren't. I didn't think they liked taking orders from a clerk—you didn't become an associate until you passed the Bar exam—but I informed them she was going to be my right hand.

Olivia sat in my office, sporting a business suit I hadn't seen her wear before. I'd expected her to come in with stacks of notes and files, but all she had was her phone.

"You got everything on there?"

"Yup," she said. "All the interrogatories. The complaint, the answer . . . pretty much everything. And it's easy to search and find something. I think those days of lawyers carrying boxes of documents into court are over."

"The boxes were usually filled with copies of the same document. It was a show for the clients to make them think we were prepared." I checked my watch. "Let's go. Judges hate it when you're late."

We took my car down. The West Jordan District Court was an L-shaped building with metal detectors up front, and three floors of clerks' offices and courtrooms. The first floor was nothing but clerks, the second was juvenile court, and the third housed the criminal and civil courts. Gills was on the third floor and off to the left when we stepped off the elevator. Before going in, I closed my eyes and took a deep breath. I opened the door for Olivia and said, "Remember one thing above anything else: if you say something confidently enough, people will believe you. Even if you're wrong."

We stepped inside the courtroom. The defense was already there— six of them, with Bob at the head. He was still wearing his eye patch. I sat at the plaintiff's table, and he said, "Morning, Counselor. You look nervous. No need to. This will be quick and painless."

I ignored him and looked up at the judge's bench. The courtroom had no windows, and it was always, somehow, cold—even in the summer. The bailiff stood by the judge's bench and stared out at nothing. When the judge's clerk came out, everybody stood before realizing he wasn't the judge. Everyone sat back down. Then the judge came out, and we had to stand again, as if we were praying to a deity.

Gills was a short man, maybe five three, maybe less. He sat on something to make him appear taller, and I wondered if it was a phone book. He looked out at our table, then over at the defense table. "We're calling the case of Joel Whiting versus Pharma-K Pharmaceuticals. Now is the time set for scheduling conference. I have before me a motion to excuse the plaintiff's presence due to health reasons. Mr. Walcott, you don't have an objection to said motion. Is that correct?"

"Actually, Judge," Bob said as he rose, "I think it's only fair that the plaintiff be here. Mr. Rucker is here and has to take time off. I'm certain Mr. Whiting wouldn't have too much trouble making it down for the court appearances."

I rose to my feet. "Mr. Whiting is a twelve-year-old boy in renal failure, Your Honor. He couldn't come here any more than he could climb Mount Everest right now."

Bob said, "I just want what's fair, Your Honor. It seems unfair that Mr. Rucker has to take time off from his busy schedule overseeing the operations for Pharma-K, and Mr. Whiting won't even have to appear in court. I think the plaintiff should have to bear the burden of filing suit."

"He's sick, Bob," I said, trying to bore a hole through him with my stare.

"Then maybe he and his mother should've thought of taking the more-than-generous offer that was made."

"Gentlemen," Gills said, "calm down. Mr. Walcott, you're being an asshole. I don't like assholes in my courtroom. Is that clear?"

"Of course, Your Honor. Again, we just want what's fair."

Olivia cleared her throat and stood up. Her hands were trembling. "Um, Your Honor, I'm . . . um, Olivia Polley, I work with Mr. Byron. I'm allowed to appear under Utah's third-year practice rule as I—"

"Ms. Polley," the judge said, "you see this chair? It's not comfortable. Hurts my ass like sitting on a jagged rock all day. Just tell me what you're gonna tell me."

"Well, I was just thinking that a good compromise might be that we excuse both Mr. Whiting and Mr. Rucker. That way no one is inconvenienced but the lawyers."

"Nothing I love more than inconveniencing lawyers. My order on the motion is that Mr. Whiting is excused for all future court appearances, and anybody the defense would want to bring is excused, as well. I'm fine going forward with just counsel at all future appearances. Everybody happy?"

"Yes, Your Honor."

"Yes, Judge."

I leaned over to Olivia and whispered, "Nice." She blushed and had to fight back a smile, as though you weren't allowed to smile in a courtroom.

"Good," the judge said. "Now, I assume we want a discovery timetable?"

"Actually, Your Honor," Bob said, "may I approach?"

"Certainly."

Bob laid a document down on the plaintiff's table then gave another copy to the judge. It was a 12(b)(6) motion.

The motion was named after the rule of civil procedure that governed it. The caption read: FAILURE TO STATE A CLAIM UPON WHICH RELIEF CAN BE GRANTED.

Bob was claiming that we didn't have any legal basis for filing a lawsuit. It was one of the most dangerous motions in all of civil practice. If the motion was granted, the suit would be dismissed, and I would find it extraordinarily difficult to bring another one. If the motion was denied, Pharma-K would likely raise the initial offer and try to settle the case. The motion was typically filed after discovery was completed, not before.

"You sure you wanna file this now?" the judge asked.

"Yes, Your Honor."

"Okay, it's your rodeo. Mr. Byron?"

"I'll need at least a month for my reply, Your Honor."

"A month it is. Get a new date from my clerk."

After we secured new dates, I asked Olivia to get started on the reply. Bob had filed one of the few motions that would allow the judge to make a decision based completely on the actual documents rather than any testimony. The judge would hold a hearing and ask us questions about the motions, but by then, he would have already made up his mind. It was a way for judges to make sure they weren't overwhelmed with crappy lawsuits. They didn't like letting things go forward when they knew the plaintiffs were holding out to find better evidence later. It was very likely this case would be dismissed in a month. So I decided I had better find something good to put in that reply.

---

I spent the rest of the workday conferring with KGB about the case, then went out to Greens to actually see where they kept the children's medicine.

Greens was one of those little neighborhood groceries that had just a few shelves of products and a couple of cashiers standing up front with nothing to do. One smiled at me but said nothing. I strolled around for a little bit, getting a feel for the place, before heading to the pharmacy area.

The over-the-counter medications were right in front of the cashier. I doubted anyone could do anything to the medicine without someone seeing. The Pharma Killer still could have either taken the bottle to another section of the store, put the poison in and resealed it, or taken it home, poisoned it, then resealed it. The first child was made sick the day before Rebecca bought the medicine, which meant her bottle likely couldn't have been tampered with the day she bought it. It had to have been the day before or the day before that. I made a note in my phone to have a laboratory test Rebecca's bottle for any glue that might prove it had been resealed.

Of course, Rebecca Whiting's instincts could have been right, meaning the medication had been contaminated at the source before going out. Pharma-K had recalled the product so quickly, I wasn't surprised there weren't more than just the three cases.

"Can I help you?" the cashier asked.

"Yes, actually. I, um, am interested in some cough medicine, but that whole Pharma Killer thing has me kinda spooked. Not sure what to buy."

"I've been hearing that a lot lately. It's up to you, but I might suggest trying another brand if you're concerned about that."

"Would that help?"

"Certainly. The contamination only affected the Pharma-K brand."

"Really? That seems weird that some psycho would just pick that brand."

He shrugged. "Well, I don't know. I can't really speak to that. What I can tell you is all the medication is right here. We inventory them every night."

"Huh. That doesn't sound like you think it was a single person." I stepped closer and glanced around, as though I were saying something controversial. "You think it could've been tainted by the company?"

"Well, I don't know. But I will say it would be very difficult for someone to tamper with one of our medications. They'd have to purchase it, tamper with it, and then put it back. And we do inventory every night. If we had one too many, we would've noted that—and we never did."

I nodded. "Sounds like there's more going on than the public gets to know, huh?"

"I would say that's accurate."

"Well, I think I'll pass. Thank you for your help."

"You bet."

I left Greens and texted Jessica to list the Greens cashiers as witnesses to depose later on.

# 19

That night, I drove home without any music. I felt like thinking. I reached the stop sign by my house and stopped. Up east was the hospital. Again, I had an urge to go up there, though I didn't know why. Normally, after a client signed up, I did everything I could to avoid that person. New clients had a tendency to eat up all of a lawyer's time with irrelevant nonsense if allowed.

I started turning toward home, then stopped. I veered away and drove up to the hospital.

Joel was awake when I got there. Rebecca was out in the hall, knitting. I sat next to her.

"How is he?"

"He threw up a lot today. He's really tired, poor thing."

"I won't stay long."

"No, he likes you. You can stay as long as you like."

"You knit?"

"Need something to occupy the time."

She kept knitting, and I watched her for a moment before I rose and peeked into Joel's room. He was just lying there, staring at the ceiling. I pulled up a chair and sat down. He smiled when he saw me. He looked much worse than he had two weeks ago. The dark circles under his eyes had turned black, and he looked thinner.

"That girl, the one that's a twin, she's cute. She been down here lately?"

He grinned. "No."

"You like her, huh?"

"She comes down and plays music for me sometimes. She really likes the Killers."

"Oh, yeah? I don't think I've ever heard 'em."

"You wouldn't like them."

"Why, 'cause I'm old?"

"No, I see you liking classic rock. The stuff my mom listens to."

"I'll have you know, Mr. Whiting, that I was pretty hot stuff when I was your age. I had the denim jacket and the Bon Jovi T-shirt that all the girls dug. I even had a Walkman that was always strapped to my hip."

"What's that?"

"It's the equivalent to rocks and sticks for you, but at the time, it was a cool way to play music." I noticed the TV was on, but the sound was turned off. "How you feeling today?"

"I can't eat or drink anything. I keep throwing up. I miss pie. My mom makes apple pie with ice cream."

"You'll be eating it again in no time."

He took a few labored breaths. "I wanna go outside one more time."

"You're going to go outside a lot. There's no rush."

He looked at me. "I'm dying, Noah."

I didn't know what to say. It was hard to be a kid after realizing you were going to die. Much harder still was knowing it was going to happen soon.

"They won't let you outside?"

He shook his head slowly. "No."

"Well, I'll tell you what: what time you wake up in the morning?"

"Like nine or ten."

"Okay, I'll be by around nine or ten tomorrow."

"What are we doing?"

I rose. "It's a surprise."

---

When I got home, I showered, then sat on the couch and tried to watch a Lakers game on the television. I couldn't concentrate. So I got a beer out of the fridge and went onto the balcony. I stared out over the city and the bright headlights of the cars coming up the road. I heard a click from next door and looked over. On their balcony was my neighbor, Jim. He was a retired professor from the University of Utah.

"You still up?" I asked.

He blew out a puff of smoke. "Not much difference between night and day when you're retired."

"That sounds like buyer's remorse."

"Worst mistake I ever made. I should've been teaching until I died. I loved those kids." He blew out another puff of smoke. "How you doin'? I haven't seen you around lately."

"Just a big case I'm working on. That Pharma Killer that's been in the news."

"They caught him?"

"No, we're suing the company that makes the medicine."

"What for?"

"I think the medicine was contaminated before it went out, and they covered it up."

He whistled. "That is a doozie if it's true." He paused. "You're too young to remember, but doctors used to smoke in hospitals. Sometimes, they'd recommend it to patients. You can still see the ashtrays that are bolted into the walls at the U of U hospital. The cigarette companies were so powerful, they convinced doctors to poison their patients."

"Aren't you smoking right now?"

"No, it's weed. You want some?"

I chuckled. "No thanks."

"Now that sounds like a man who needs a hit. Hang on. I'm coming over."

The front door opened half a minute later, and Jim walked in. He sat on the deck chair next to me, packed a pipe, then handed it to me. I took it.

"I haven't smoked this stuff since college."

"It's for the young and the old, but you sound like you need it right now."

I took a small puff, and it gave me a hacking cough that made Jim laugh. I leaned my head back and watched the stars.

"So who's your client?"

"A little boy who got sick, Joel Whiting."

"He okay?"

"No. And those dicks are gonna get away with it like it never happened."

"Well," he said, taking another puff off the pipe, "nothing's written in stone."

# 20

In the morning, I bought two pairs of scrubs and texted Olivia to meet me at the hospital. Then I rented a van from Enterprise and drove up to the hospital parking lot. I saw Olivia sitting in her car, waiting for me. I got out and handed her one package of scrubs. I was already wearing mine.

"What is this for?"

"Go to the bathroom and change. Then meet me by the elevators."

"Why? What's going on?"

"We're busting out a prisoner."

When I'd first approached Rebecca about this late the previous night, she hadn't even hesitated to say yes. She had been trying to take Joel out for weeks, but the doctors wouldn't allow it.

I grabbed a wheelchair from the front entrance, then waited by the elevators. Olivia came out wearing scrubs, her clothes in her hand. I pushed the button, and we went up to ICU. Rebecca was already waiting in front of Joel's room. Her eyebrows rose when she saw our outfits.

"I don't know about this," she said.

"We won't do it if you don't want to."

She thought for a second. "No, let's go. Hurry up, the nurses are all hanging out at the nurses' station."

We went into Joel's room. Olivia helped me lift him into the chair. He was so light, she could've done it herself.

"Where we going?" he asked.

"Surprise, remember?"

I pushed him down the hall, Olivia walking next to me, trying to act as casual as possible. Though the nurses had to buzz people into the ICU, they didn't buzz anyone out. We quickly went through the double doors leading to the elevators.

"Noah," he whispered, sensing we were doing something naughty, "where we going?"

"You'll like it. Trust me."

We got on the elevators and went to the main floor. Hurriedly, we left the hospital and loaded the wheelchair into the van before all of us piled in.

"Where are we going?" Olivia said.

I just grinned as I pulled out of the hospital parking lot.

---

About twenty minutes from Salt Lake was an amusement park called Lagoon. Even from a mile away, Joel saw it and turned into a four-year-old kid. He squealed, and the look on his face as he stared out the windows at the giant roller coasters was something I'd never seen. In an instant, he changed in a way that adults may have forgotten was possible.

We parked and helped him down the ramp. Rebecca and I had talked last night and decided riding the roller coasters was too dangerous, so I hoped I could still show him a good time without riding the actual rides. His mother held his hand as we walked to the front of the amusement park, a smile so wide on Joel's face I thought it might hurt his cheeks.

After I got the tickets, I pushed Joel in his wheelchair, and he talked about the last time he was there. He'd thrown up cotton candy on one of the roller coasters that turned riders upside down.

We played some of the carnival games, and he tossed softballs at milk bottles to knock them down. His throws were too weak to get the ball far, but he didn't seem to mind. The sunshine, the people, and the excitement were enough. He wore a smile from one ear to the other.

A ride called Rocket Mouse occupied one end of the park near the kids' section. Joel kept asking his mother if he could ride it. She said no, then he said, "But Noah will ride it with me. Right?"

He looked at me, and I just nodded. As far back as I could remember, I had never ridden on a ride at an amusement park.

The rocket was two seats, and Joel sat in front of me. It was a kids' ride and didn't go very fast, but he still turned to me and said, "Don't worry, it won't make you sick or anything." He whistled to his mother, letting her know he was okay, and she whistled back.

The ride took off, and we spun up into the air, then leveled out. The entire rocket tipped upside down—I hadn't been told that would happen—then spun right side up again. Joel was howling with laughter, but I felt the slow rise of pressure from my stomach into my throat. I swallowed as the rocket spun again.

By the end of the ride, I must've looked green, because Olivia was laughing when she helped me out of the rocket.

"You poor thing," she said. "I think you better not go on any more rides with him."

The next ride, Olivia took him. They were both laughing and screaming like toddlers. When they stepped off, Joel held her hand. It was a casual gesture, a little thing that showed his affection, but I watched her eyes and saw them well up with tears.

Joel asked for cotton candy, and his mother bought him some. He had a couple of bites, and that was all he could handle. He was sweating profusely.

"I think it's time to go," Rebecca told me quietly.

We'd only been there for a couple of hours, but when we left, Joel looked exhausted.

"Can we come back tomorrow?" he asked me as I wheeled him out.

"I think I'm going to still be vomiting from that mouse ride tomorrow."

We loaded up in the van and headed back to the hospital. Joel fell asleep on the way over.

---

I hurried to the office after the hospital and had Jessica send out subpoenas and schedule depositions for me. I didn't know where the Pharma-K employees were going to be in a month, and I wanted to get them on record. And if I was going to overcome Bob's motion, I needed as much evidence attached to my response as possible.

Jessica and I scheduled the first depositions quickly, which was surprising. I'd assumed Bob would fight me on it, schedule them at odd times, then reschedule at the last minute several more times—a common defense-firm tactic.

Instead, we had five depositions scheduled for the next day. Two of them were executives at Pharma-K—one was the head of quality control, and two were employees in the warehouse. It was unheard-of to schedule that many depositions in one day. The most I'd ever done in one day was two. That made me nervous. Had Bob already put the fear of the Almighty into them, and were they just going to clam up and not tell me anything? Or maybe they had been coached from the beginning to outright lie. Whatever was going on, I didn't trust what they were going to say tomorrow or the few days afterward that I would have them if I needed more time. I texted KGB and asked if he could be there, and he said he could. If they lied to me, he could follow up, and we could have them called out on perjury in front of the judge. Witnesses weren't allowed to lie during a deposition any more than they were during a court hearing.

I prepared an outline of my questions. The great thing about depositions was that there was no judge there to tell anyone to hurry. I could ask about anything and take all the time I wanted. I had to pay a court reporter or stenographer to take notes and a videographer to film it, and sometimes, I had to fly out to wherever in the country the witness was, but that didn't apply to this case. Everyone I needed was right here.

I looked up in the evening and saw Marty standing by the door.

"You okay?" I asked.

"It's this Pharma-K case. I'm not comfortable with it."

"Why?"

"It's something about it. I know, I was the one who pushed you to look into it. But I think you're getting too attached."

"Too attached?"

"You told me once that the worst thing for a lawyer was to be attached to a case or a client. That it clouds your thinking and you can't think of the bottom line. I see it happening with this."

"See it happening how?"

He came into my office but didn't sit. "Noah, I've seen you talk clients into taking deals they swore up and down they would never take. You didn't take the million dollars, because you're internalizing this case."

I sighed and leaned back in the seat. "I think they know a helluva lot more than they're telling us."

"Every case has a victim. And sometimes, we don't get to win. We compromise so that both sides can move on. This company's not going anywhere, and even if they did, Joel would still die. It doesn't help anything by fighting this out over the next few years and blowing our money on it. He's still gonna die. I'm sorry, but you need to accept that and detach yourself from it."

"That's what I've done my whole life, man. Detach. Detach from my parents, from my friends, from my wife . . . detach so I can focus on money. That was the only thing that mattered."

"It's still the only thing that matters. There are almost seventy employees at this firm relying on you, Noah. They put food on the table with the money you bring in for them. They dress their children and pay their insurance because of you. That's not valueless. Focusing on the money is important. Don't forget that."

I watched as Marty left. Then I swiveled my chair around and stared out at the sky. The sun had nearly set, with darkness coming quickly behind it. I wanted to leave, to go somewhere outside. A park maybe. Or the canyons. And even as I thought it, I knew I wouldn't go. I turned back around and continued writing questions for the depositions. I worked faster than I had before Marty came in, and I didn't know why.

# 21

That night, I stopped at the stop sign again. I let the driver behind me honk several times before he swerved around me and flipped me off. Finally, I headed toward the hospital.

Rebecca was asleep in Joel's room. She was on the recliner, a blanket covering her. Joel was asleep, too. I stood at the door, which was open, and I was about to leave when Joel whispered, "Noah?"

"Yeah," I whispered back.

"What're you doing here?"

"I, ah . . . I don't actually know." I leaned against the door frame. "Just thought I would pop in. Get back to sleep, though. Sorry I woke you."

"Thank you," he said quickly as I turned to leave. "Thank you for today."

I nodded. "You're welcome."

As I was heading out, I stopped at the nurses' station. A nurse with short blonde hair was sitting at a computer, typing away. She didn't look up when she said, "How can I help you?"

"Do you know much about transplants?"

She looked at me. "Why?"

"I was just curious about how they decide someone can get an organ transplant. I mean, who's the guy on that? The final say?"

"Well, it's actually a program we have. The algorithm takes into account something like a hundred different variables and tells us if the potential recipient should be transplanted."

"A computer decides whether people are going to live or die?"

"Well, we don't think of it that way. The doctors and counselors have the final say."

"And the insurance companies."

"Yes, whether someone can afford it is a huge factor."

"What are the variables the algorithm uses?"

"Oh, a lot of different things. Age, occupation, other diseases, are they drinkers or smokers, income—"

"Income?"

"Yes. People with higher incomes tend to be able to take better care of transplanted organs."

I grinned and shook my head.

"Something funny about that?" she asked.

"No, it's just that the law has a similar formula to determine what someone's worth. It screws the poor, too." I looked back to Joel's room. "He's a good kid."

"Joel? Yeah. He reminds me of my son. It's so sad seeing him go through that every day."

I exhaled. "Thanks for your time."

---

When I left the hospital, I wasn't sure where to go. I didn't feel like going home. I texted Olivia.

*Have you eaten yet?*

*No.*

Within a few minutes, I was at her house, and she was walking out. She got into my car, and the smell of her perfume hit me. It wasn't overpowering; it was subtle, almost as if she were embarrassed to be wearing any.

"That was really sweet of you to take Joel out today," she said as we pulled away from her house.

"I've never actually been to Lagoon."

"Really? But you've been on roller coasters and stuff, right?"

I shook my head.

"Wait a second. You've never been on a roller coaster?"

"No. My dad would never take me anywhere, and by the time I could go on my own, I was too old."

"Our stamps on our hands are still good. Go there now."

"For what?"

"That is like the saddest thing I've ever heard. We're going there right now to get you on a roller coaster."

"Olivia, it's fine. I just want—"

"No, we're going. Right now. I never got to go either. I was always at home taking care of my mother. We're two people who have never been on a roller coaster, Noah. We can't let that stand."

I rolled my eyes and turned the car around. It seemed pointless, but if that's what she insisted on doing—well, it was better than sitting home alone.

Lagoon looked a lot different at night. All the rides were lit up with multicolored lighting, and the people, mostly adults, were squealing and screaming on the rides. We went inside, and Olivia put her arm around mine. She led me to the first roller coaster we saw—the Skycoaster. As we waited in line, she didn't let go of my arm, and I was glad.

We got on the roller coaster, and I felt butterflies in my stomach.

"You okay?" she said.

"Yeah. Why?"

"I think you actually look nervous. You don't even look nervous in court."

"I'm fine."

The roller coaster jolted forward and began a slow climb. We seemed to climb right into the night sky. The higher we got, the more silent it became. We were at least two hundred feet in the air, and I could look down and see everyone walking along in the amusement park. I could see the freeway beyond the parking lot, but I didn't hear the traffic.

And then, in an instant, it was done. The roller coaster reached its apex, then rocketed downward. My stomach jumped into my throat, and Olivia screamed. I tried to hold it in, but I couldn't help it—I hollered, too.

The roller coaster twisted upside down, then did a hard right before doing a hard left and spiraling upside down again. It sped up, then stopped suddenly, throwing everybody forward. My heart was pounding, and I couldn't get the smile off my face.

"See, everybody likes roller coasters," Olivia said as the car pulled back in to the platform.

"Let's go again."

---

We rode rides until the park closed at midnight. Then we got giant fruity drinks in glasses the shape of trumpets and sat on the curb as people left the park. I watched her, the way she looked at people. She didn't look at them the same way I did. Something was different in the way we approached the world, and it came out in the way we viewed people. She saw them with this bright look in her eyes, like each person had the potential to be a friend. I didn't see them that way. Perhaps the opposite: each one was a potential new enemy.

"I used to get so jealous of the other kids in high school," she said. "How they got to do stuff like this and I couldn't." She leaned in and kissed me on the cheek. "Thank you for taking me."

We sat on the curb a while longer, until almost everyone had left, then we strolled to my car and leaned against it, talking about nothing that seemed important. Time slipped away and when I realized how late it was, I kept it to myself because I didn't want this day to end.

When I dropped her off at her house, all we said was good night. I watched her walk to the door. If she turned around, just one glance, I'd know she felt the way I did. All it would take was one glance.

*Just one glance. That's it. Just one. Come on . . . come on . . .*

She got to her door and unlocked it. Before the door shut, she turned around and smiled at me.

"Yes!" I nearly shouted.

I waved to her, and then drove home smiling the entire way.

# 22

The next morning, I wore a black pinstripe suit with a gold Bulova watch. I slicked my hair back Gordon Gekko style—I didn't have any real heroes as a kid, and I'd had to find them in the movies I watched. Gekko had style, ruthlessness, and above all, money. I wanted all of that.

We usually held depositions in our own conference room, but Bob requested we do them at the Walcott offices. Home-field advantage and all.

Walcott's office was in the most expensive building in the city. It took up an entire floor, and it was a throwback to the old Wall Street law firms from the sixties, who only wanted Ivy League grads that were white, Protestant, and came from money. Though the Walcott partners claimed they didn't discriminate, the firm had exactly one black attorney and one female attorney. And they had managed to find both traits in the same person—Gale Nest, who was actually far too nice to be working in a firm like Walcott. As I waited in the lobby for Bob, I saw her walk by. She waved and came over.

"When you gonna leave these pricks and come work for me?" I asked.

"I'm not ready to chase ambulances yet."

"Oh, please. Insurance companies came up with that so people wouldn't come to us."

"Maybe. But it's not bad here. I think everybody's scared I'm going to sue if they treat me poorly."

"They're soulless, Gale."

"Look who's talking."

Olivia and KGB stepped off the elevator together. I told the receptionist we were all here, and she called back, then said they were ready for us.

"Think about it," I said to Gale.

We headed back to one of Walcott's massive conference rooms. Five attorneys, a stenographer, and a videographer took up a corner of the table—no witnesses. They must be in a separate room so they didn't hear anything the attorneys were saying.

I sat down across from Bob, and KGB grabbed a chair in the corner. Olivia sat next to me. I pulled out a digital recorder and hit Record.

"Morning, Bob."

He smirked. "Let's just get started, shall we? I expect a long day with all these witnesses."

I put my hands on the table. "I'd like to start with Caroline Rhees."

"Mrs. Rhees, unfortunately, has transferred branches. She is now in our Hong Kong plant."

"Since when?"

"A couple of weeks. It was her decision. I'm afraid she's not available for deposition."

I held his gaze a second. "Fine. I want Michael Sulli."

"I'm afraid Mr. Sulli has turned in his letter of resignation and moved back to his home state of Iowa. He is unavailable for deposition."

I looked over at the lawyers sitting by Bob. They wore smug expressions on their faces, as though they were dealing with trash and giving it what it deserved. They didn't see injured people behind this suit. They didn't see people at all.

"Robert Rakes."

"I'm afraid Mr. Rakes has resigned from the company." Bob looked at one of the other lawyers. "I believe Mr. Rakes took his last bonus check and moved to California, did he not?"

"He did, sir."

I looked at the last two names on my list. "Heather Chang or David Pettit."

"I'm afraid Ms. Chang and Mr. Pettit are no longer with the company. I believe they, too, have moved out of state."

I leaned back in my chair and turned off the digital recorder. I ran my finger across an itch on my forehead. "You're wasting time, Bob. If that kid dies, this becomes a wrongful death suit rather than a negligent injury suit."

"We can handle anything you throw at us. Now, are we done here? Would you care to schedule some more depositions?"

I glanced at Olivia. I could see KGB in the background, and he shrugged.

"I want everybody," I said.

"Excuse me?" Bob replied.

"Everyone. I want to depose every single employee of Pharma-K."

The lawyers laughed, and Bob looked at them like a parent about to discipline a child in front of his friends. They quickly stopped laughing.

"Do you have any idea how long it would take to depose—"

"I don't care. I want every single one. Expect subpoenas on all of them." I rose. "Fire all of them if you can."

We left the firm. On the elevator ride down, I turned to KGB and said, "Find Debbie Ochoa. Whatever it takes."

---

I spent hours at the gym. I did sprints, played basketball, lifted weights, took a cycling class . . . anything to exhaust my body and take my mind off the case. Bob had declared absolute war. He had let me know today that there would be nothing cordial about this case. I hadn't expected him to be friendly, but firing employees so they couldn't be witnesses was something I'd never seen before. I had no doubt the employees had all received large severance packages in exchange for going quietly and moving out of state. I would have to find them all and grill them about the deals they received. They'd probably signed nondisclosure agreements, but it was illegal to dodge a lawful subpoena. Which meant the NDAs wouldn't be valid.

I didn't blame Bob. I knew he was doing what he had to so he could win. But he didn't understand me, and he didn't understand that I would do whatever *I* had to.

After the gym, I sat in my office. I had pulled two more paralegals from other divisions and tasked them with doing nothing but drafting and sending out subpoenas to Pharma-K employees and setting up times for the depositions. I wanted everybody: janitors, secretaries, website developers . . . I didn't care if they'd ever stepped foot in the company offices or not. I didn't care if they lived out of state or not. We would serve the subpoena, and if they couldn't come to Utah, we would fly out and depose them or pay for their ticket back.

Marty came into my office and shut the door. He paced in front of my desk for a few seconds before saying anything.

"This isn't good, Noah."

"What isn't?"

"Do you know how much this is going to cost us? Raimi thinks if everyone is here in the state, it will still cost us almost two hundred thousand dollars in witness fees, stenographers, and videographers, not to mention the transcripts we'll have to make afterward. Each transcript is three hundred bucks a pop. For over four hundred employees! And that's not counting the ones who live out of state."

"I don't care."

"Yeah, you don't care, but maybe the rest of us do. We've never spent that much on any one case, and we're not even to the first motion yet."

"Marty, calm down. I got this."

"Really? Do you even know what you're looking for? Do you have any idea? You still don't know if there actually was any negligence on their part. This is insanity, Noah. Stop this now."

I shook my head. "I'm going to win this case."

"Why? Because you want to?"

"No," I shouted, "because I'm the best. I'm the fucking best at what I do, and I'll be damned if fucking Bob Walcott gets to push us around."

I stopped and immediately felt stupid for yelling. Marty just sighed, then leaned down over my chair and looked me in the eyes.

"This is ego for you. I told you, you're too attached. You're too involved in this case. If you really believe in it and don't want to let it go, fine. Give it to me. I'll work it, and I'll get them a good settlement. But you need to get off this case."

"I can't."

"Why not?"

"Do you remember that case we had the first year we were open? The guy that got sideswiped by that truck."

"Ray something. Yeah, I remember. Why?"

"I wanted to settle and take that first offer. It was a lot of money to us at the time. Six figures. It seemed like all the money in the world. But you said not to take it. Do you remember why?"

He exhaled loudly through his nose. "I said my gut told me something was wrong with him."

"And it turned out our client's rib had splintered and some of the fragments got into his heart. We settled for five times what they offered us. It was your gut. That's all we do, Marty. We have spreadsheets and damages tables, we got economists and actuaries who work for us, but really it's just our guts. My gut's telling me something is really wrong with this. Something's just under the surface, and I need to find what it is."

He shook his head. "This is different. This is personal for you. That case wasn't personal for me. It was a calculated risk. This is emotional."

We looked at each other for a moment, then he straightened up and said, "Noah, there's three of us. Majority rules. It's not to that point yet, but it can be. I don't want to do it. I want all of us to feel like we can pursue cases we're passionate about. But I won't stand by and tell those seventy people relying on us that they're out of a job because we were passionate about one case."

He left the office, the echo of his words bouncing off the walls. I sat for at least ten minutes afterward. Maybe he was right. If I was too close to this case, I wouldn't be doing Joel or his mother any favors. Not to mention our firm. I didn't know what to do. I picked up the phone and hesitated a second before punching in the number. Tia picked up on the second ring.

"I was just thinking about you," she said.

"Nothing bad, I hope."

"No, not at all. I'm on the beach right now and I thought of the first time you tried to surf."

"Is that what you call it? I only remember it as the time I almost drowned."

She laughed. A soft, sweet sound that I hadn't heard in years. It took me back to a time when it seemed like it was us against the world. I pushed the thoughts out of my mind and turned around, watching the sky out of my windows.

"Have you talked to Rebecca?" I asked.

"Yeah, actually. She called to say how awesome you are. She said God sent you to them."

"Yeah, I think they actually believe that."

"She's always been religious. The whole church thing was lost on me. I didn't see the point."

"Maybe the point is that you have somewhere to turn when you don't have anywhere to turn."

"That doesn't make sense."

I rubbed the bridge of my nose, feeling the dull ache of a coming migraine. "I don't know if I should stay on her case. Marty's telling me I'm getting too attached. That I can't see the case for what it's worth."

"What do you think?"

"I think something horrible happened, and if we settle, we'll never know what it was."

"Then you have your answer."

"Yeah, but what if I lose us a bunch of money and end up screwing over Rebecca in the process? They offered a million dollars and I told her not to take it. That's a great settlement for this case."

"Noah, if there's one thing I know about you, it's that you will fight with everything you have to get what you want. If you really want more money for them, you'll get it. That's why I sent her to you. I know you won't let her down." I heard a man's voice in the background. "Better go. We're getting on a cruise."

"I wish I could've taken you on one. I know you always wanted to go."

"Good-bye, Noah."

I bit my lower lip as I hung up, then let it roll against my teeth before leaning back on my seat. I wouldn't be withdrawing from this case. Marty was just going to have to toughen up, because I had a feeling it was about to get much harder.

# 23

I had one case on my calendar—a black-and-white slip and fall, which I transferred to one of our associates. Joel Whiting's case was now the only thing I had to work on. Olivia, four attorneys, four paralegals, and two law clerks were also on the case. It quickly became apparent that I would need at least six more attorneys to handle all the depositions. I couldn't do 426 depositions by myself.

I pulled the attorneys from other divisions. This would mean that their cases would get transferred and the firm would have to decline new cases coming in to those attorneys. I didn't hear any grief about it from Marty or Raimi, but when they saw me in the hall, I could see it in their eyes. They were scared.

Our firm had three million cash on hand. Personal injury wasn't like other fields of law, where the clients paid up front. We worked on contingency, which meant that we could sign up a case, spend twenty thousand dollars on it, and not see a dime back for eighteen months.

Our cash on hand was how we stayed in business and kept financing cases. If our funds dropped too low, we would either have to stop taking cases altogether, just to pay salaries and operating expenses, or start firing people.

I left that night after examining the deposition lists we'd made. Most of the depositions, upwards of ninety percent, I guessed, were not going to give me anything. They were the people keeping Pharma-K up and running, but they had no say in any decisions. I didn't expect them to give me anything, but I still sent the subpoenas.

I didn't talk to anybody on my way out of the office. I got into my car and drove around the city for a bit. I stopped at a free concert in a park and rolled down my windows. A band led by a beautiful Latina woman jumped around onstage. A harp player and a sitar player sat quietly near the drummer while the woman and guitarist ran from one side of the stage to the other. The music sounded like rolling water, violins and electric drums, and before long, I realized I'd spent half an hour just sitting there.

My phone pinged with a text from Olivia just as I looped up toward my house.

*Hey. What're you doing?*

*Just going home. What are you doing?*

*Still at the office. Want to meet up for a drink?*

*Sure. Blue Door?*

*Okay.*

The Blue Door had started downtown as a pub and somehow transformed into an upmarket wine bar. Cops staked out the area around it, pulling over people randomly and hoping to bust a drunk driver. DUIs were big moneymakers for the city. The fines and fees paid by the defendants kept the city courts going and paid the salaries of the police officers and prosecutors on the cases. It was a weird symbiotic relationship that I wasn't sure either side actually realized was happening.

Inside, the bar pulsed with its evening crowd. I took a table by the windows and ordered a light red, something French. I didn't feel like drinking, but I didn't want to sit there with an empty table, either.

Everybody was laughing and having a good time. I saw starving college students wearing scuffed shoes and rich old men in two-thousand-dollar suits—the whole gamut of the socioeconomic spectrum. Though everyone appeared to be having a good time, something about their body language was off, like being there was cover for the loneliness they actually felt. I got the distinct, frightening impression that none of them were really happy. Was this where I was going to end up?

Olivia was dropped off by a cab and came in with a smile on her face. She sat down across from me and ordered a Sprite before putting her elbows on the table and leaning toward me. A smile crossed her lips, giving me that odd mix of nausea and excitement I used to get when a pretty girl smiled at me in grade school.

"I'm sorry," she said.

"For what?"

"For today. For this case. It must be hard trying to decide between money and helping a friend."

"What friend?"

"Joel is your friend, Noah."

I shook my head. "He's a client. It's different."

"I'm not sure it is." She scooted up on the chair, making herself more comfortable. "I'm getting some angry calls. People are seriously pissed that we're subpoenaing them. A lot of them are saying they don't know anything about the poisonings."

"They're scared. Anyone reveals anything incriminating, and the company will retaliate. Probably sue them as well as fire them. Under Bob's advice, of course." I took a sip of the wine. It was sweet, as though it'd been mixed with juice or something. I pushed it away from me. "How's your mom?"

"Good. That's nice of you for always asking. You should meet her tonight."

"I'm not exactly the guy you want to take home to Mother. Parents don't usually like me."

"Bullshit, she'll love you."

She blushed, and I knew she hadn't meant to swear. She was getting more comfortable around me, maybe not seeing me as a boss. I didn't want her to see me that way, either.

"The test for the glue came back this afternoon," I said. "No glue on the bottle Joel's mother bought. Means it wasn't resealed."

"That's good, right? I mean, it's less likely someone tampered with it."

I nodded, staring down into the crimson wine. "Marty wants me to give him the case."

"Are you going to?"

"I don't know. I think it might be the right call. He'll get it settled, and we'll be done. Rebecca can move on with her life."

"She's never going to move on. Joel is her only child. There's nothing out there for her after this. It might just be a case to us, but to her, it's her entire life."

"Why do I get the feeling you're trying to talk me into keeping the case?"

"Because I know you'll fight for it."

"So what if I do?"

"From what I've seen, these Pharma-K guys are scumbags. They hurt children and don't care one bit about it. Those kinds of people will hurt others again. They're the insurance adjusters that knew a sixteen-year-old girl couldn't fight for her mentally ill mother, so they refused to pay. I don't think Marty cares about that."

"You've got it backward—I'm the cold-blooded one."

She didn't respond, but her smile told me she wasn't convinced. She saw something in me. Something I didn't see.

I ordered a couple glasses of white wine as we talked, then I had to have Olivia drive. We went to her house—a small home on the west side of the city in an area known for little more than crime and industry—and she said, "Come in. My mom's still awake."

I followed her up the lawn and into the house. It was a quaint house, like a discontinued model that had gone out of style, but I liked it. It smelled like herbs, and the carpets were clean. It was quiet, completely still. In the kitchen, Olivia flipped on the light, then got a couple of sodas out of the fridge and handed me one.

We sat down at the dining table and talked. She told me how studying for the Bar was going, who she got along with at the office, and who she didn't get along with. I just listened. She sounded so . . . young. It seemed like as most people grew older, the world made them cynical. That hadn't happened with her, yet. I got the impression that she was actually shocked that people working together couldn't get along. Something only the young believed wouldn't happen.

She was only seven years younger than I was, but she was from a different generation—one that seemed somehow entitled, but entitled in a good sense of the word. Her generation knew they were supposed to do well and expected it. I didn't know if that would help them or hinder them in the long term.

A woman wearing a bathrobe came in, looking frail. Her hair was the same color as Olivia's, and her face looked worn and tired, but the intelligence that enveloped Olivia shone there, too. Long, thin fingers sat on hands that appeared too thin to be healthy, with trimmed and polished nails. I pictured Olivia sitting on a bed with this woman, trimming and polishing away at her nails as though it was the most normal thing in the world for an adult to be doing. And I felt sorry for them both. Sorry that Olivia had missed her youth to take care of the person who was supposed to take care of her, and sorry that her mother probably understood the pain she had caused her daughter.

She smiled weakly at me and said, "Olivia, who's your guest?"

"This is my friend Noah, Mom."

"Hello, Noah."

"Hi, Ms. Polley."

"Jan is fine." She went to the cupboard and got down a bottle of pills. She placed two in her mouth, then took a sip of water. "How do you know Olivia?"

"We work together."

She began walking out of the kitchen. "Isn't that nice."

Olivia seemed embarrassed. "Sorry, she's not much of a talker."

"She seems sweet."

"Can't choose our parents, right?" she said. "I sometimes wonder what my dad was like. I didn't know him at all."

"Sometimes it's better not knowing. But if you could trade, would you?"

She took a sip of her soda. "No, I wouldn't. I love my mom. When she has her moments of clarity, I can come to her for advice, we watch television together . . ." She grinned. "The other day she even asked when I was going to give her grandkids."

"When are you?"

"That is the furthest thing from my mind right now. What about you? Do you want kids?"

"I don't know. I don't know if I'd want to bring them into this world. It seems like it's getting darker rather than lighter."

"The world's always been a mess. You can't change that. You just have to straighten out your little corner of it."

"So I take it you do want kids one day?"

"Lots of them. I don't want a minute of silence in our house. Might drive my future husband nuts, but he'll have to learn to deal with it." Her face grew somber. "This house is always quiet. It's been quiet for twenty years. I don't want that for my kids."

"My ex wanted kids. The marriage fell apart before that happened, though."

"You've never talked about your divorce."

"There's not much to talk about. Sometimes, people just grow apart. I was focused so much on building the firm, she got the sense she wasn't the most important thing in my life. If you're going to do that, to commit fully to another person and swear to them that you're going to spend the rest of your life with them, I think they have to be the most important thing to you. I feel terrible for the things I put her through. I can't even imagine how lonely she must've been when I was choosing to work eighteen-hour days. She deserved better." I twisted the soda in my hand. "What about you? Ever come close?"

"To marriage? No. I had a serious boyfriend in college, but he took off because of my mom. I think he saw the writing on the wall that we come as a package."

I hesitated before saying, "There are homes that can take care of her."

She shook her head. "No, I can't do that to her. They would treat her like a paycheck. Just wheel her in front of a television and forget about her. I won't do that. She's my mom, and she needs my help."

"You know, sometimes, not often, but sometimes, I daydream about my dad coming and finding me. That he asks for help. And I wonder if I would."

"You would."

"You don't know that."

"I do. You don't seem like the type of guy who wouldn't help if he could."

She didn't say anything else, but she reached across the table and laid her hand gently over mine. Her fingers warm and soft. I stared at her hands, the smooth skin and the nails, and then moved my hand so that it was holding hers.

"Well," I said, "I better go."

She nodded. We stared at each other for a second, then I rose from the table. I had the impression that if I'd wanted to stay the night, she wouldn't have objected, but I didn't want that from her right now. That was odd for me because that seemed to be the only thing I had wanted from women ever.

As I got up to leave, she kissed me on the cheek.

"I'm sorry," she said. "I know you're my boss and all."

I couldn't help but grin. "Good night, Ms. Polley."

"Good night, Mr. Byron."

I had that familiar feeling of nausea and excitement in my gut again as I walked to my car.

# 24

The next couple of weeks were a flurry of activity. All the depositions had been set so that I could attach them in my reply to Bob's motion for dismissal if I found anything good. We'd subpoenaed four former employees in California, two in Hong Kong, two in Texas, three in New Jersey, one in Iowa, and one in Washington. The rest were, luckily, current employees located in Utah. I pulled four more lawyers from other divisions in the firm. They would be the ones flying around.

A few times a week, I went to the hospital to see Joel. I started buying DVDs of movies he wanted to see that they didn't have at the hospital. We would watch them until he fell asleep, then I would sneak out and head home. Most nights, I couldn't sleep, so I worked on the questions I wanted to ask in the depositions.

The first deposition was on a Friday. We got through two of them that day. The next Monday, I got through two more, then another four on Tuesday and Wednesday.

Most of the witnesses were people who knew almost nothing about Pharma-K: the lower-level employees who didn't even realize Pharma-K's product was involved in the scandal. I got exactly zero relevant information from them. Until Wednesday, when I deposed a factory worker named Dan Atkin.

We conducted the depositions in my firm's conference room this time, and Bob was there with three other attorneys. Defense litigation firms that represented corporations and insurance companies billed by the hour for each attorney. I estimated Walcott was making about twelve hundred dollars per hour from the depositions. That was one of the reasons Bob hadn't fought me or gone to the judge when I'd subpoenaed every employee. He wanted us to have hundreds of hours of depositions: we lost money, and he made money. In hindsight, I could see that Marty had a point.

Dan Atkin wore a denim jacket and looked about as nervous as someone could look. Olivia, a paralegal, and I sat on one side of the conference table, and Bob and his crew sat on the other. KGB was also there, billing at two hundred fifty per hour. We also had a videographer and a court reporter who swore people in and acted as a stenographer. The true cost of all this suddenly hit me, and I didn't know if I had set all this in motion because I'd thought it would give us something or if I'd just been angry in that moment with Walcott.

"Name, please," I said.

"Daniel Atkin."

"You live here in Utah, Mr. Atkin?"

"Yessir, down in Pleasant Grove."

"How long have you lived here?"

"I dunno, twenty-some-odd years."

"How long have you worked for Pharma-K?"

"Three years."

"And what do you do there?"

He swallowed and looked at Bob as though he would be giving away too much information by answering that question. "I, um, load the trucks."

"What do you load onto the trucks?"

"When the products are ready to ship, I'm one of the loaders. I load up the trucks, and they go out to the pharmacies and stores here in Utah. We do our own shipments to save money so we don't have to hire no one. We do that in every state with a plant."

"Were you at work on April sixth of this year? It was a Wednesday."

"Yessir."

"Do you remember loading Herba-Cough Max children's medicine?"

"Yessir, I believe we did. I only remember because when this whole thing happened, I thought back about it."

"And some of those shipments went to Greens Groceries, up there on 1300 East?"

"That is one of the places we deliver to, yes."

"Who had access to that medicine before it was delivered?"

He made a puffing sound. "Shoot. Everybody, I guess. Anyone in the plant."

"*In* the plant? So no one outside the plant could've had access to that medicine?"

He looked at Bob again, and Bob didn't say anything. Atkin's cheeks flushed red.

"Well," Atkin said, "I don't know. I'm not there all the time. I just come load the trucks and then drive 'em. I'm rarely at the plant."

"You just said anyone in the plant would have access to the medicine. You implied that someone outside of the plant wouldn't. Right?"

"Well, like I said, I don't know."

"If someone outside the plant wanted access to the medicine before packaging, how would they get it?"

"I . . . guess they'd wait for the bottles before they were sealed. Wait for it there."

"How would they get inside the plant?"

Atkin was clearly flustered now. He kept wringing his hands and looking to Bob for help. Because the exchange was being videotaped, Bob couldn't help. He knew I might play this tape for the jury down the line. But Bob glared at Atkin with squinted eyes, a look that let him know he'd better tread carefully in what he told me.

"Well, um . . . I don't know. We got security guards that check our badges and scan 'em, and no one but the designated employees are allowed on the floor. Even our lawyers aren't allowed on the floor. Just the people that work there."

"So it'd be almost impossible for someone who wanted to get into the plant from the outside and tamper with the medicine to do so?"

"I don't think anything's impossible, but it'd be hard. He'd have to forge an ID and then make sure it scanned right into the computer. I don't see how someone could do that."

That was all good information—nothing dispositive, but good information. None of it did anything to help the primary theory Pharma-K was putting forth, that someone had poisoned the medicine at the stores. But I had guessed it would be tough for someone to get into the plant. That meant the cough syrup had to have been poisoned by someone at the plant or while it was at the store or on the way to the store.

I asked Atkin another hundred questions, all meant to lull him into repetitive boredom: Where did you go to school? How did you get hired at Pharma-K? Who's your boss? How did he or she get hired? How long has he or she been there? Are you married? Did you go to college? What did you study? What medications are you on?

I wanted him to be bored. People lower their defenses when they're bored.

After a little more than a hundred useless questions, I asked the one question I really wanted to ask Dan Atkin—the one I could've asked and ended the deposition with from the beginning.

"Any cyanide in the plant that you know of?"

Dan opened his mouth and was about to answer when Bob snapped out of his near sleep and said, "I'm objecting to that."

"On what grounds?"

"On the grounds that it's irrelevant."

I chuckled. "Whether the poison found in your medicine is in the area where you make the medicine is irrelevant?"

"It will paint a picture for the jury that is entirely unfairly prejudicial. Don't answer that, Mr. Atkin."

"He can answer that, or we can get the judge on the line."

"So get him."

I exhaled. "Jessica, please get Judge Gills on the line."

A few minutes later, the judge was on speakerphone.

"Morning, Your Honor," I said. "We have a little dispute during one of the depositions that I was hoping you could help with."

"What is it?"

I could hear the aggravation in his voice. We were adults, and judges expected us to work through our own problems until trial. Considering this was an adversarial process where neither side trusted the other, I never knew why judges thought that would be the case.

I explained the situation, and the judge said, "Mr. Walcott, what did I say about assholes in my courtroom? That applies in depositions, as well."

Bob's cheeks flushed red. "Your Honor, that question is loaded specifically to—"

"Holy shit, can you two not agree on anything? Mr. Atkin, please answer the question. Your lawyers may object to its introduction at trial, but you have to answer it during this deposition."

Atkin said, "What was the question?" before taking a sip of water. He was stalling.

I said, "Is there any cyanide at the plant, or was there any cyanide at the plant at any time?"

He looked at Bob, who narrowed his eyes.

"I, um . . . yes."

My guts felt as though they'd been dipped in ice water. I looked at Olivia, then back at Dan Atkin. He was staring down at the table, unable to bring his eyes up to mine.

"Where is the cyanide?"

"We don't . . . there isn't any there anymore."

"What was it used for?"

He mumbled something.

"Mr. Atkin, you are under oath, with a judge listening to your answer. What was the cyanide used for?"

"Rodents. We had mice or rats or something. We used a treatment."

"What kind of treatment?"

"Pills and a liquid. Capsules, I think. They were laid out in the corners of the plant."

"Are they still there?"

"No."

"When were they removed?"

He shrugged. "I don't know. I came in, and they were gone."

I looked at Bob, and he was just staring at Atkin.

"Was the rat poison there before April sixth?"

"Yes."

"How soon before?"

"I don't know. A week, maybe."

"What brand?"

"It was called X-Zero One. It's a rat and mice killer."

"And how do you know it contains cyanide?"

"I was the one that bought it."

I stared at him quietly. "Who told you to buy it?"

"One of my supervisors, Karen. She said to go out and get some and then provide the receipt to her for repayment. Then she had us put it all around the plant."

"Did you tell the police this? That there was cyanide in the plant?"
He shook his head. "No, the police never interviewed me."

It was true. The investigation on this case had been atrocious. If the local police weren't competent enough to handle it, they should have called in the FBI sooner, but that call hadn't been placed until Joel was already in the hospital. I didn't have access to the FBI reports yet, but it was increasingly important that I get them.

"Why didn't you tell anyone?" I asked. "You saw the news stories, right? Why didn't you tell anyone that you knew your company had rat poison lying around in the same plant the medicine was manufactured in?"

His gaze seemed to drop lower, and he shrugged.

# 25

After the judge got off the line, I grilled Dan Atkin harder than he had ever been grilled in his life. We were there until midnight, then we came back the next day and didn't finish until eight at night. I went through every possible thing that could've gone wrong at Pharma-K with the rat poison: who knew about it, who had handled it or might have handled it accidentally, where he purchased it, who removed it, and where it had gone once it was removed. I grilled him about rats. Was it possible a dead rat with cyanide in its blood could've gotten into the medicine? I even asked him to draw a map showing where he'd placed the poison and where he'd seen dead or dying rats.

I was dragging the information out of him until about the eighth or ninth straight hour. By then, he was so exhausted that he just gave me what I wanted, hoping I would stop.

At the end of the second day, none of us had our suit coats on. A lot of bottled waters and sandwich wrappers cluttered the tables. Our sleeves were rolled up and ties loosened. I asked Atkin questions until my throat dried and burned. Bob objected dozens of times, and several times, we had to call Judge Gills. One time, I thought I heard his wife in the background say, "Come back to bed, you idiot. We're not done."

When the deposition was over, we had recorded nineteen hours of Dan Atkin's testimony. Those nineteen hours would have to be pored over and analyzed, then transcribed and analyzed again. Atkin looked as though he had run a marathon. He didn't have the strength to do anything afterward but leave without talking to anyone.

Bob waited until everyone had cleared out but him and me. He rose and went over to the windows.

"When I was a boy," he said, "I knew I'd be up here one day. In the towers looking down on everyone else. I knew even then there were people who went about their lives in blissful ignorance, holding to ideals and principles as if they would somehow save them. As if ideals mattered. But I also knew that there were other types of people. People who saw the war we had engaged in from the minute we became self-aware. They did what had to be done. Abraham Lincoln gutted the constitution of this country worse than almost any other president, but he's revered as the greatest American who ever lived. He's revered because he did what he had to do for the greater good."

He turned and faced me.

"Pharma-K is the greater good. They're the Google of start-up pharma companies. All the top young minds in the field want to work for them. Billions of people will benefit from their innovations. Billions. That's why I do what has to be done to protect them. They are the greater good, and you are the blissful ignorant."

I leaned my head back on the chair. "Every dictator in history has made that same speech, Bob. Hitler thought he was fighting for the greater good, too. Isn't it odd that the most defenseless always need to be the ones sacrificed for the greater good?"

He leaned on the conference table. "What if you're wrong? What if you're wasting valuable time that could be spent investigating and catching the psychopath responsible for poisoning that medicine? What if more children get sick because Pharma-K was defending this lawsuit and its public image rather than investigating what happened?"

"If there is such a man, the FBI's gonna find him. Not you."

"The FBI can't put a dump truck full of money out there to find someone. We can."

I didn't reply. What he said was true. They could put out a reward of a million dollars for information leading to the man responsible—if there was such a man. But because of pending litigation, it would be wiser for them not to take any action. Everything they did at this point would be scrutinized by a jury, and I could paint their attempts to find the killer in whatever light I wanted.

I saw a helicopter fly around a building and over the valley, and I watched its blinking lights for a few moments.

"That's what I thought," he said. "You don't know if you're wrong. You don't fully buy your own bullshit. Take the million dollars, Counselor. Take the million and have your client never talk about this again. It's the best she's gonna get."

He walked out of the conference room, leaving me alone, staring out at the night sky.

The next night, I found myself at the stop sign again. Every muscle in me screamed for sleep, but I knew I couldn't. I had to be at the hospital. I drove up there and parked before heading down to the cafeteria, where I bought an energy drink. I guzzled half of it to keep me up, then sipped at the other half as I walked to Joel's room.

The videographer was already there. He was setting up the equipment while Rebecca spoke to someone on her phone.

Joel had lost even more weight. His hair looked thin and greasy, and strands of it had fallen out over his pillow. I sat down next to him. His breathing was labored and raspy.

"Hey," I said.

He grinned, but it was slow and weak, as if he couldn't muster the strength for a full smile. "Hi." He motioned toward the nightstand. "Look what I had my mom bring."

I glanced over. *Select Works of Lord Byron.* The book was thick and still had the glossy cover of a new copy.

"Wow," I said, picking it up. "I haven't seen this for a while." I flipped through a few of the pages. "Do you understand it?"

"Not really. Some of them don't make sense."

"That's the beauty of poetry," I said. "That language is inadequate to describe life. So poetry just tries to bring up emotions. Just read it and see how you feel. If you feel something, then the poem worked."

The videographer, the same one who had done the depositions, said, "We're ready."

I looked at Joel a moment. "You ready to talk?"

He nodded.

The video began to record. Joel swallowed and had so little body fat on him I could see the full movement of his throat. He opened his hand. I stared at it, then I reached up and held it.

"My name," he rasped, "is Joel Whiting . . ."

# 26

I had trouble sleeping for the next couple of weeks. The video, just under ten minutes long, kept replaying in my head. Joel looked sicker every time I saw him. He was on dialysis every day now, and the whites of his eyes had tinted a light yellow from the jaundice: his liver was failing, too.

I also interviewed the nurse who had initially admitted Joel, the one who'd run to his house to get the medicine. She was an older lady, Bettie Thyfault, but one with a happy disposition that likely came from loving what she did for a career.

"I knew right away what it was," she told me in her deposition. "I'd read the story that morning about one of the other boys, and I just knew there'd be more. The mother was hysterical, so I got her keys and went to the house. I brought the cough medicine back to our lab and had it tested." She shook her head. "That poor boy. Lightning has to strike somewhere, though, doesn't it?"

"This wasn't an act of God, Ms. Thyfault," I said, staring right at Bob. "What happened to Joel didn't need to happen." I finished the deposition and let her know I might call her to testify at trial, and then spent the rest of that day reading transcripts from depositions I'd already conducted.

I turned to the clock: a little past midnight. We had made it through only 197 depositions, and the 12(b)(6) hearing was tomorrow. Every scrap of information we could pull together had been attached to our reply on the motion. It brought our reply up to 137 pages. Gills, I figured, would lose focus after about fifty pages or, worse, only read the headings, subheadings, and conclusions, completely ignoring the evidentiary facts we'd managed to scrounge up.

The total bill for the depositions had risen to $275,000 so far. I was now using eight attorneys, eight paralegals, and three law clerks, who couldn't do anything else. Considering the lost revenue from other cases those lawyers could've been working—and some of them could have been billing hourly on divorces or other cases—Joel Whiting's case had already cost our firm around $500,000. We'd spent about fifteen percent of our total cash on hand.

Though it was late, I threw on a pair of shorts and a T-shirt and headed up to the hospital and sat in the hallway across from Joel's room. The nurses no longer enforced visiting hours for Joel.

The door opened and Rebecca, bleary-eyed, stepped out of the room. A look of surprise came over her.

"Sorry," I said. "Couldn't sleep."

"It's okay. I was just heading down to the cafeteria to get some juice for him. He's awake right now if you want to go in."

I nodded. She walked past me and gently put her hand on my shoulder before heading down the hall. I rose and entered the room.

Joel had his eyes closed. I sat down in the recliner against the wall and watched him. Each breath seemed to be a fight. When his chest rose, it looked as though he had forced it up, as if each inhalation was a conscious act because his body had already stopped working.

Slowly, his eyes opened, and he looked at me, a slight grin lifting his face.

"If you're tired, I can leave."

"No. I want to talk. Some of the medicines I'm on make it hard to sleep."

"We have a big hearing on your case tomorrow. If we win, they'll probably make a big settlement offer. If we lose, the case is over."

"If we lose, then my mom doesn't get anything?"

"Afraid not."

He thought for a second. "I'm scared, Noah. My mom will be all alone."

"She seems like the kind of lady who can take care of herself. You just work on getting better. I'll take care of your mom."

"You'll check in on her and make sure she's okay?"

"Yes, I will."

He exhaled forcefully and tilted his head back up, his face toward the ceiling. We were silent for a couple of minutes.

"What's it feel like to kiss a girl?" Joel asked.

I grinned. "It's like . . . if you take everything fun that's ever happened to you and you wrap it up in a ball and put it on your lips, that's what it feels like. You can feel her heart beating against yours, and it seems like the rest of the world disappears. You don't remember what you have to do tomorrow or anything like that. It's just you and her."

He smiled. "I thought you were gonna say it's wet or something."

"It can be that, too."

We listened for a few minutes to the hum of the machines and a quiet conversation in the hospital room next door.

He swallowed. "Do you think my daddy's waiting for me in heaven?"

I looked away. I felt something in my throat and sensed that I couldn't talk right then, so I was silent for a long time. "Yes, I think your daddy's waiting for you."

He did one slow nod. "I think so, too."

We didn't say anything for a while, then Rebecca came in. She helped Joel sit up and then gave him his juice. A nurse came in a little bit after that and checked readouts on the machines. The nurse gave him pain medication. Then he drifted off slowly. I rose and went to his bed. Looking down on him—he was so frail—I wanted to do something. It was insanity that this boy had to lie in this bed when I had money: the lifeblood of the world. Something could be done. Someone, somewhere, could help him.

His hand moved, and it drifted across the bedsheets toward my hand. He held it, his touch like a small child's. He also held his mother's hand, and the two of us stood there while the machines carried on in their soft beeps.

# 27

I woke up and realized I had slept at the hospital. I was lying on the recliner in Joel's room. I stood up and quietly snuck out of the room while he slept, Rebecca in a chair next to him. I rushed home and threw on the first suit that I saw in my closet. The hearing started in twenty minutes.

Taking the freeway, I zipped in between cars and got there in fifteen minutes. I passed the metal detectors, bolted up to the courtroom, and went in just as Judge Gills was taking the bench. Bob was already there, with four other attorneys, one of whom was Gale Nest. Someone must've told Bob that I'd talked to her, and he decided having her on the case might provide some advantage.

I sat down at the plaintiff's table by myself. Raimi and Marty were in the audience seats, but I didn't ask them to join me. Only Olivia, who must've been out in the hall or the bathroom, came up without being asked and sat next to me. She reached under the table, grabbed my hand, and squeezed as she smiled, as though letting me know that whatever happened would be okay.

"All right," Gills said, "you bastards ready to go?"

"Ready, Your Honor," Bob said.

"We're ready," I said, standing up.

---

The hearing lasted an hour. Gills went through the main points, but I very quickly picked up what he was looking at: he wasn't sure there was a link between Pharma-K's negligence and the poisoning, despite Dan Atkin's deposition testimony.

We had made several document requests, asking for emails or intra-office memos pertaining to the rat poison and anything else relevant. As was customary for insurance company and corporate defense firms, when we asked for five or ten documents, they sent thousands. One hundred fifty-two boxes had showed up at our firm, and we'd had to put most of them in a storage unit. The emails I wanted were in there, somewhere, but we would have to go through another two hundred thousand documents to find them. I had three paralegals sifting through the documents full time, and we still hadn't found any emails pertaining to the rat poison.

Bob countered that every company with a building in that district used rat poison because of the rodent problem and that we hadn't presented a shred of evidence that the poison had gotten into the cough medicine at the plant.

Judge Gills was quiet, only occasionally asking a question, then letting us argue it. Bob and I went back and forth until he finally said, "Okay, I've heard enough. You'll have my ruling tomorrow."

We left the courtroom, Olivia holding my hand. Raimi and Marty clearly noticed, and they exchanged glances. We didn't speak until we were outside.

"You did an awesome job," Olivia said.

Marty slapped my shoulder. "Top-notch, buddy."

I looked at Raimi. He was incapable of flattery. "What do you think, Raimi?"

"I think it's a close call. The judge could side either way, and he wouldn't be wrong."

We agreed to meet up again later that afternoon to go over contingencies. If the motion was granted, then we needed to prepare a media statement so we didn't look like idiots to the public. If the motion was denied and the case was allowed to carry forward, we needed to decide how much to settle for.

---

I couldn't eat—my guts were in knots—so I went back to the office. The FBI reports relating to the Pharma Killer were on my desk now. The investigation by the feds hadn't added anything other than a couple of extra interviews and a better timeline of when everybody had known what. The most interesting part was that their Behavioral Science Unit had come up with a profile of the Pharma Killer.

The profile said he would be white, in his mid-thirties, possibly living with his mother or grandparents, with a string of firings from menial jobs behind him. He might have a genius-level IQ but not one person in his life he could consider a friend. The profiler had called him a cowardly killer who needed to distance himself from his victims because he didn't have the fortitude to see the harm he'd actually caused. I looked up the agent online: he had been profiling cases for less than a year, and he didn't have a degree in psychology.

The reports included notes about an ongoing FDA investigation, as well. The FDA consisted of people who had worked for the meat and dairy industry or the major pharmaceutical companies, and people who wanted to work for those companies. A typical career track consisted of gaining ten years of experience at the FDA, then getting a high-paying job in one of those industries. Anyone who wanted one of those high-paying jobs would have to make rulings against those companies for violations of the law—that almost never happened unless they were investigating a smaller company. That relationship set up a system in which the people who were supposed to be watching out for consumers were actually the consumers' biggest threat.

The FDA reports said they were testing other products for contamination, but I was certain they weren't going to find anything.

I was about to take a break and go to the gym when my phone rang. I hit the intercom button and said, "Yeah, Jessica?"

"Judge Gills's clerk called. He has a decision and would like both counsel there."

# 28

Apparently, Jessica had called everyone, because within ten minutes of arriving at the courthouse, I saw Raimi, Marty, several other attorneys from our firm, and Olivia. She came up to the plaintiff's table with me again and sat down. Bob was there, still wearing his eye patch, along with all his other attorneys. He looked over at me and winked.

"That was quick," Olivia whispered. "What does that mean?"

I shrugged. "It means we either won or lost."

"All rise," the bailiff hollered, "Third District Court is now in session. The Honorable Judge Nathan Gills presiding."

The judge hurried out. "Sit your asses down, Counsel." He leaned back in his chair and groaned. "All right, let's get to it. We on the record yet?"

The clerk nodded.

"Okay, Mr. Byron. It's weak. You're assuming there's negligence because some people got hurt without having any actual link to the company. You're hoping the jury will be moved by emotion and ignore the fact that you don't know exactly what happened, because no one knows exactly what happened."

Bob grinned at me. He looked like a cat about to eat a mouse.

"And, Mr. Walcott," the judge said, "the very poison that harmed those children just happened to be lying out on the plant's floor ten feet from where the medicine is made. I don't believe in coincidences. Not to mention the fact that the little tidbit about cyanide being near the medicine was not disclosed to law enforcement during the investigation, and the rat poison just happened to disappear days after the injuries were reported. It stinks to me. I don't know which way I would rule on this yet, but I know some more discovery needs to be done. I'm denying defense's motion to dismiss. My clerk will set up a trial date and discovery schedule that works for everybody. Thank you."

The judge rose and left. I sat there, stunned, still processing the words. I only realized we had won when I looked at Bob and saw he had turned a furious red. I looked behind me, and Marty came up and shook my hand.

"I was wrong," he said.

"You were right," I said, and clapped him on the back. "Remember? You told me to take the case in the first place."

Marty, who had known Bob longer than I had, went up to him and spoke quietly. Probably rubbing a little salt in the wound. I turned to Olivia.

"You did it," she said.

"I haven't done anything yet."

The bailiff approached us. "Counsel, the judge would like to see you and Mr. Walcott in chambers."

Bob, Olivia, and I headed back with the bailiff to the offices behind the courtroom. Judge Gills's office had a window, a couch, a desk, and almost nothing else. I didn't see a single photo of his wife or children.

We sat down and Gills rubbed his stomach, a grimace on his face.

"Damn gas," he said. "Don't get old. That was the advice my father gave me. I wish I would've listened."

"Your Honor," Bob said, "frankly, I'm a little surprised about your ruling."

"I'm sure you are," he said, reaching for a bottle of antacid in his drawer. He popped two in his mouth and chewed loudly. "The ruling's made. But I didn't like it. I liked it more than if I'd ruled the other way, but I don't like this case. Bob, your client's acting shady. And Mr. Byron, your case is shit. This needs to settle. I'm not taking up eight weeks of my time and a jury's time on shit. What's the current offer?"

Bob said, "One million."

"Mr. Byron, that sounds like a fine offer considering the question of liability."

"I think we can get more from a jury, Your Honor."

"Not with all the bullshit caps we have on punitive damages in state court. What did your client say?"

"She'll do what I advise her to do."

"Bob, offer more."

Bob smiled placatingly, but I could see anger behind the smile. "Judge, it's not the bench's position to even discuss settleme—"

"Oh, cut the shit. Offer more and be done with it. I have a trip coming up and don't want to be stuck here listening to you two scream at each other like teenage girls. You offer more, and Mr. Byron, you tell your clients how far you are from liability and get them to take it. Everybody's happy."

"That twelve-year-old boy who's going to die isn't happy," I said.

The judge and Bob stared at me. I held the judge's gaze and then said, "Is that all, Your Honor?"

"Yeah, that's it."

I rose and walked out. Bob followed me. "Don't be stupid, Noah. I'm going to take the judge's advice. You should, too."

"He wants this case to settle so he can go on vacation. He doesn't give a shit about my client."

"You think you're the only one who cares that a child got hurt? You're not. We're all just looking at it more objectively than you are. Once you've lost your objectivity, it's time to get out."

"That is such bullshit!" Olivia blurted. "I looked at your client's stock last night. It's dropped fifteen percent since this story broke. That's what this is about. You don't care about Joel."

We both looked at her and she blushed. To her credit, she didn't back down this time. She held Bob's gaze like a pit bull about to be unleashed on a rival.

"I see it's not just you who's lost objectivity at your firm," Bob said. "Take the damn money. Or I swear to you, they will get nothing, and that boy is still going to be dead."

# 29

When I got back to the firm, everyone had gathered in the reception area. They clapped when I stepped through the doors. The Commandant brought out a cake with a money sign on it. People began shouting, "Speech, speech."

I still didn't know exactly what had happened. I had gone into that hearing absolutely expecting to lose. I mumbled a few words about never giving up and fighting tooth and nail, then we cut into the cake. I slipped away to my office as soon as I could. I stared out the windows, the adrenaline still coursing through me and making me jittery.

"Hey," Olivia said from behind me. "Marty's out there saying they're gonna settle this case for at least three million. Is that true?"

I shrugged. "They'll make a big settlement offer. Winning the motion will be in the news, and the board of directors for Pharma-K will order Bob to make it go away as quickly and cheaply as he can. The families of the other two boys retained lawyers, too. They were waiting to see what happened today before filing suit, but they'll do that now. They'll get settlements, too."

"So I guess we won."

"Guess so."

"What did Rebecca say?"

In the rush, I had completely forgotten about telling Rebecca. "I totally forgot. I'm going to head up there now."

She hesitated, then leaned in and kissed me on the lips. It was soft and quick. Then she pulled away, tucked a strand of hair behind her ear, and left me there, my heart still pounding.

---

I reached the hospital around noon, passing crowds of doctors and nurses eating lunch in the cafeteria. I took the elevators up to Joel's room. Rebecca was outside, crying.

"What's wrong?" I said.

"Joel stopped breathing. He stopped breathing, and they're . . . and they're . . ."

I didn't wait for a response. I went to his room and saw the doctors working on him. I stood there until someone pushed me aside and ran in. So many people were in there, crowded around his hospital bed, that I couldn't actually see him. I sat in a chair next to Rebecca as she sobbed.

---

An hour went by before we got word that Joel was breathing on his own and his blood pressure had stabilized. We weren't allowed to see him yet. I stayed in the chair next to Rebecca and turned off my phone. Marty kept calling me. Bob had probably called the office in an effort to settle the case quickly. Bob could wait.

I went to the cafeteria and hung out there for a while. I got a soda and sat at one of the tables, listening to people's conversations, the way I had as a new lawyer looking for clients. But now I didn't want them as clients, and I actually listened to what they were saying. Entire lifetimes were recounted there. People reminisced about things that had happened long ago, because the future was uncertain, and all they had was the past. A lot of pain was there, but I heard a lot of joy, too. I had never heard either when I was looking at them as potential clients.

At one point, after I returned to the hallway, Rebecca fell asleep and put her head on my shoulder. We sat there like that until Dr. Corwin came to speak with us.

"You can see him now, if you like," he said.

Rebecca got up and went into the room, but I stayed. I stood and faced the doctor squarely, watching as Rebecca ran in and sat down next to Joel, running her hand over his head.

"How much time does he have?" I said.

"Not long. He's in stage-five renal failure, the end stage. The patient doesn't typically die from the kidneys directly but from sepsis or heart failure. I've been working with his hepatologist, and Joel's also in liver failure."

"How long?"

Dr. Corwin couldn't look me in the eyes. He licked his upper lip, which was dry, then looked down at his shoes.

"Doc, how long?"

"Couple of weeks. Maybe just a week."

I rubbed my forehead. "I know what this is about. I know how the world really works. So let's not play with words. Let's be honest about it. You get him a new kidney, and tomorrow, I will cut a check to this hospital for half a million dollars. A donation. Think how much good the hospital could do with half a million dollars."

The look on the doctor's face told me he pitied me. He put his hand on my shoulder. "Even with a new kidney, his liver will kill him. Money doesn't fix everything. I'm sorry, Mr. Byron, but that boy is going to die."

# 30

I drove around for hours. I drove as far as the canyons near Sundance, then walked the grounds, watching people hike up a trail to a mountain. I sat by the stream for a while and watched the fish before I headed back into the city.

I had to settle the case quickly. I wanted Joel around to see it. I wanted him to know his mom would never have to work again. That meant I had maybe a week to do everything. But I also wanted something else, something from Pharma-K that didn't involve money, and I wasn't sure what that was—mostly because I had never wanted it before. Somewhere, deep in my gut, I wanted to fight.

I rushed back to the office. It was well after hours, and most people had gone home. Marty was still there.

"Bob's called three times," he said.

I sat down in his office. Unlike me, Marty had pictures everywhere, mostly of his brothers, sisters, and now, Penny.

"You gonna ask her to marry you, like you said?"

He nodded. "You betcha. Next month."

"That's great. I'm happy for you."

"What's the matter? You should be ecstatic, Noah. We got a huge check coming in. I was skeptical, but that's the last time I do that. I'll never doubt your instincts again."

"I don't wanna settle."

He stared at me. "Sorry, it sounded like you said you don't want to settle."

"I don't want to settle. Tell Bob we're going forward with the trial."

"Why the hell would we possibly do that?"

"Just tell him, Marty."

"No, I will not tell him. And neither will you. We're taking whatever new offer they make. Do you know how much we're into this case already? Five hundred grand. Trial might be three times that. We're taking their offer."

I shook my head, but my voice was even and calm. I didn't have the strength to put up a battle. "It's my case. I'm not taking any offers." I stood up. "Tell him we're going to trial."

I went to my office and sat down. My back hurt from sitting in hospital chairs, and I stretched it from side to side. Then I leaned my head back and closed my eyes. The door opened a few minutes later, and Raimi and Marty came in. They sat down across from me.

"I'm not taking an offer," I said. "You won't change my mind."

They glanced at each other. Marty said, "We're not here to change your mind, Noah. We're here to tell you this is no longer your case."

Now they had my attention. "What do you mean?"

"I mean we're taking a partners' vote. And Raimi and I vote that you are off this case. You're no longer allowed to talk to the client or to opposing counsel. It's not your case anymore."

I laughed. "You're shitting me. You guys are really gonna pull that with me?"

"Sorry, but this isn't about you. It's about the firm and protecting our bottom line. You are off the case."

"Like hell! I'll call Bob myself and tell him."

"I've already spoken with Bob," Marty said. "I've informed him that you have been taken off the case and that all settlement negotiations will go through me. I told him you no longer speak for the client and do not have authorization to negotiate any offers."

I shook my head. "After everything I've done? I built this damn firm."

Marty just looked at me sadly. "And so you think you can destroy it? A trial will cost us too much money. We can't do it."

"We will win, Marty. We will fucking win. I guarantee it."

"Sorry, but we're not willing to take that chance. You're off the case."

The two of them rose and left the room. At the door, Raimi turned and looked at me.

"Raimi, you can't be with him on this. He's getting married soon and I get that he wants security and isn't willing to—"

"I've run the numbers on this case a dozen times. Joel Whiting is just not worth that much."

I shook my head. "That kind of thinking, Raimi, is what Bob Walcott does."

"We deal with rational approximations, not emotions. We can't do it. Taking this to trial goes against every principle we founded this firm on."

"Well, what if we were wrong?"

"I'm sorry you think that. You'll see that this was the right decision in time."

He gave me a sympathetic look, then shut the door, leaving me alone.

# 31

The next morning, I heard the news: Pharma-K had settled the case. Olivia texted, asking why I hadn't been at the negotiations. She told me the company would be paying the Whitings 2.4 million dollars. Of course, the family would have to sign a gag order. Marty was up at the hospital, discussing it with Rebecca right now.

I didn't get out of bed until noon. When I did roll out, I put on a robe and sat in the living room, watching movies, something science fiction, then a couple of dramas. I ordered a pizza. I ate that and some old ice cream I didn't know I had. The ice cream was freezer burned, so I melted it a little in the microwave, then mixed it with whipped cream.

Then I sat on the balcony and smoked a cigar. I leaned back and looked over the city. The sun reflected in sharp angles off the glass buildings, big trucks rumbled on the freeway in the distance, and the smog seemed to cling to the sky like dirt on skin. I slowly finished the cigar, then lit another. I kept glancing over at my neighbor's house, hoping to see Jim, but it didn't look like he was there.

I got up, threw on some sweats, then sat back down on the couch. I texted Jessica and told her I was taking the rest of the week off and to clear my calendar.

The next day, I did almost the same thing. I didn't answer emails or phone calls. Olivia texted, saying that the paperwork was being drawn up and the deal was being signed tomorrow. However, Rebecca had accepted the two million dollars only on the contingency that I tell her personally it was the right thing to do.

Once we subtracted all our up-front costs and took a third of the settlement, she would still have over a million dollars left—a good settlement on a case where negligence on the part of the company wasn't a slam dunk and the victim was a child with no earning capacity. She would never have closure—that was a myth—but maybe she could get remarried and provide a good life for any other children she had. That would be Joel's legacy: to provide for siblings he would never meet.

I slept all day. When I woke up, it was dark outside, and I was disoriented. I couldn't remember if I'd fallen asleep at night and woken up or if I had taken a nap and just slept in. I knew I'd taken a nap when I saw that the television was on. I never slept at night with the television on.

I was about to get dressed when I decided to turn my phone back on. I planned to text Marty and tell him I was going to the hospital to advise Rebecca to accept the money. Pharma-K would still do business as usual, and not a single person would be punished for what had happened. But I had lost. There was no point in fighting it anymore.

I went through and deleted messages. One was from KGB. He had found Debbie Ochoa, the woman Rebecca had originally spoken with at Pharma-K, who had told her the psychopath poisoning children's medicine was a story invented by the company. Debbie was living in California and wouldn't talk to KGB, but he thought if I went out there personally, I could get her to talk.

Several messages were from Olivia, checking up on me. A few were from Marty and Raimi. I had a couple from Jessica and the Commandant. One was from Rebecca. I listened only to Olivia's and Rebecca's.

Rebecca was crying. "Noah, please . . . please come down."

That was all the message said. She had left it two hours ago.

---

I raced through the hospital. In the ICU, the nurse, the one I had seen in Joel's room a dozen times, was sitting at the nurses' station, staring at a computer monitor. Her eyes were red from recent crying.

I ran down the hall. Inside Joel's room, two doctors and a nurse stood with Rebecca. She sat next to the bed, holding his hand. His breaths were labored, quick short intakes followed by a long exhalation. His eyes would sometimes roll into the back of his head.

I froze by the door; I didn't have the strength to step inside. I stared at Joel the way someone would stare at a fairy tale come to life. I had known it was coming, but I couldn't believe it was happening. My mind wouldn't let me.

"Mama," he rasped, "Mama, I was worried, but I'm not worried anymore."

Rebecca wiped away her tears with her free hand and held in her sobs. "Worried about what, sweetheart?"

"I was worried . . . I was worried how you would find me and Daddy when you get to heaven. I knew there'd be a lot of people, and I didn't know how you would find us. But I know now, Mama. I'm gonna whistle. So when you get there, I'm gonna whistle for you so you know where I am."

Rebecca's head dropped onto the sheets. Her body convulsed in powerful sobs, but she stayed silent so Joel couldn't hear her. Even now, she still thought only about him.

This was a moment she would never forget. She would think about it every morning when she woke up and every moment before she went to sleep for the rest of her life. It wasn't a moment meant to be shared with me.

"Sir, please step outside," one of the nurses said, rushing into the room.

I collapsed into a chair and stared at the hallway floor. Within an hour, Joel had slipped into a coma.

Two hours after that, Joel Whiting was dead.

# 32

I stayed at the hospital for as long as they would let me. Rebecca wouldn't leave the room, even after they had taken away Joel's body. She sat by the bed and sobbed. Finally, the nurses said that I would have to leave. They would take care of Rebecca, and her aunt was flying in to be with her. They said I should go so they didn't have to worry about me, too.

Leaving the ICU felt like a waking dream. Everything was surreal and blurry around the edges. I roamed the halls of the hospital until I found a quiet place to sit in a hallway with walls of glass that looked out over the mountains.

A hand pressed lightly on my shoulder. It was Olivia. She didn't say anything. Just wrapped her arms around me and held me. I buried my face in her shoulder. I wept, and she didn't let me go.

———————

Olivia drove me back to my house and came inside. It wasn't spoken, but I knew she would be spending the night with me. She wouldn't have left my side if I had told her to.

We watched shows and talked about things we'd never talked about before: about what she was going to do when there was no choice but to admit her mother to a home, where she wanted to go, and what work she wanted to do. She told me she wouldn't be staying at our firm. She wanted to work at a nonprofit.

"It's not the selfless world you think it is," I said. "It's grinding work. The people you do it for are rarely appreciative and the people you beg for money hate your guts. The ones who donate who don't have much money, you feel sorry for because they think they're paying to help people. Most nonprofits spend more than eighty percent of their funds on salaries and overhead."

"I don't think success or failure is the measure. It's the trying. It's doing your best to try and follow what you think is right. I thought big-firm life would be for me. I've never really had any money and that sounded appealing. To hire a full-time nurse for my mom and take her places. I've met a lot of rich people through this firm, Noah, and none of them seem happy to me. I wanna try another way. The money will barely be enough to live on, but I'm willing to take that chance."

"It's not a good decision."

"Maybe not, but it'll be my decision. Not my mother's, not society's, just mine. And if it's a mistake, it's my mistake."

She was telling me something about myself, too, but I was in too much of a haze to think about it. My thoughts felt like soup in my head, everything mixing with everything else. All I wanted to do was take a sleeping pill and hide under the covers for a few days.

"I don't know if I can go back to the firm," I said. "The thought of talking to someone who's been in a car accident and telling them how much money I can get for them makes me sick. I might be done with law."

She didn't say anything. She just took my hand and led me out to the balcony and we watched the city lights below us. After a few minutes, she said, "I'm going to tell you something I've never told anyone else." She swallowed and didn't look at me. "I lied to you."

Emotion choked her and her eyes welled with tears. I put my hand over hers and she wiped away the tears and kept going.

"When I told you about that serious boyfriend I had? He didn't run off because of my mom. I was a . . . I'd never had sex before him. We'd been dating maybe a month, and he kept hassling me about it, but I wanted to wait. One day we went out to this park and we were lying down by the stream, hidden by some trees. He, um, he started taking my clothes off and I told him to stop, but he wouldn't. He pushed my hands over my head and held me down. He started . . . he raped me. I couldn't even scream, I was in, like, shock. A deep shock where you can't even move." More tears came and she wiped at them with her fingers. "He didn't say anything after. He just got up like it was the most natural thing in the world." Inhaling deeply, she finally looked at me. "I wanted to die, Noah. That night, I wanted to die. I felt worthless. Like it was my fault. Why hadn't I screamed? Why hadn't I put up more of a fight? I didn't understand it. So I went to the medicine cabinet and got a bunch of my mom's pain pills. I had them right there, on the counter. Twenty of them. I had made up my mind and I was gonna do it."

"What stopped you?"

"The thought that my mother wouldn't have anybody. When you give up, it's not yourself you hurt the worst. It's everybody who cares about you. I would've hurt her worse than anyone's ever hurt her in her life."

She hugged me tightly and put her head on my shoulder. I could smell her shampoo and just that—the pleasant scent of another person near me, their warmth, their touch, their tears—made me realize how alone I had been. It stung in a way I didn't think it would, almost like physical pain.

"I'm so sorry you had to go through that. Did you ever go to the police?"

She shook her head. "I was too embarrassed. I thought it was my fault. By the time I realized it wasn't, it didn't matter anymore. I heard from someone else that he was already in prison for raping another girl. I went to his parole hearing a few years ago. I sat in the audience and watched him. Coward couldn't even look at me."

I held her and watched the city. I wanted to tell her that if that guy ever got out, I would kill him. But that seemed condescending some-how, so we just held each other quietly a few moments before she asked about the case again.

We talked about how KGB had found Debbie Ochoa. The one witness who could prove liability on the part of Pharma-K. Finally, we talked about Joel.

"It was money," I said. "I'm rich . . . and I couldn't save him. Every-thing I have—all my money, power, everything I fought so hard to get my entire life—it was . . . an illusion. When I needed it, nothing was there."

She looked into my eyes. "You have the capacity to help a lot of people. You won't be able to help all of them, but you will help some. It's the people, Noah. That's what matters. The people who love you and look up to you are your power, not the money. One of the asso-ciates told me Marty was bankrupt when you met him. He was going to quit law and go back to Iowa to help run his dad's hardware store. The Commandant was working three jobs to support her kids as a sin-gle mom when you paid her double what other people in her position make. I've heard all the stories. Your employees adore you because you helped these people when nobody else was there to help them, Noah. That's your power." She took my face in her hands; our eyes locked. "Fly out to California tomorrow and see Debbie Ochoa. Don't let them get away with this. That's what you fought your whole life for: to be in a place where you could help Rebecca Whiting."

Neither of us was hungry, so we didn't eat. We just went to bed. Olivia fell asleep next to me, and it was warm enough that we left the sliding glass doors to the balcony open and let the balmy air wash over us.

The next morning, I booked a flight to Los Angeles.

# 33

LAX was as crowded as I remembered. I stepped off the plane with KGB and headed straight for the car rental. He'd come along to record the interview. Attorneys interviewing potential witnesses solo could bring about a host of problems. If the witness changed what they said later, the attorney would have to testify against them, and withdraw from the case since it would be a conflict.

We rented a car and got on the freeway. KGB chewed on a tooth-pick and stared straight ahead.

"You hungry, Anto?"

"No."

"Don't talk much, do you?"

"No."

Those were the only words we exchanged during the entire drive to Santa Monica. The drive took a long time with traffic, and I turned on a Pandora station to fill the silence.

I loved Santa Monica, and I kept stealing glances at the beach as we drove toward Debbie Ochoa's condo. The sky was clear and blue. We parked in front of her duplex and I knocked on the door and waited. According to Anto, Debbie shouldn't be working right now. That made sense, considering that she had probably received a nice severance package from Pharma-K.

The door opened, and a Hispanic woman in a yoga outfit stood there. She looked from one of us to the other and said, "Yeah?"

"Debbie Ochoa?"

"Yes."

"I'm an attorney, Noah Byron. I represent Joel Whiting. He's an . . . he was a boy that had taken Herba-Cough Max."

"Was?"

I nodded. "Joel died last night."

"I'm sorry, I can't help you."

She tried to shut the door. I placed my foot in front of it and pulled out my phone. I brought up the photo of Joel making a silly face and showed it to her. "This was Joel. He was twelve. He went through about as much pain as a human being can go through before he died." I put my phone away. "Please. I just need some information."

She looked away, then opened her door wider. "Come in."

We entered the condo. Debbie sat us down on a couch with a plastic cover, and she sat across from us. The television was tuned to a Spanish soap opera. She muted it and stared at us.

"They knew, didn't they?" I said.

"I'm not supposed to talk about it."

"You told Rebecca Whiting that Pharma-K made up the story about the serial killer to cover themselves. You felt something for her then. Can you even imagine what she's going through today?"

Debbie swallowed. "I lost my baby, too. He had meningitis, and the doctors couldn't save him."

"I'm sorry. I didn't know. How old was he?"

"He was four. Eric. I was with him at the hospital every day. Rebecca told me about how she would sit and cry herself to sleep in the hospital room, but she had to do it quietly so her boy wouldn't wake up. I did the same thing."

I leaned toward her. "I'm so sorry you lost your son. I can't imagine what that feels like. But I can imagine that if someone was responsible, you wouldn't quit until they paid for what they did. I can help Rebecca do that, if you help me." It sounded like begging, and ultimately, I was.

"I can't testify. And you can't record this. If they find out I told you, they'll take everything I have. I signed contracts."

"Anto, please wait outside."

He rose without a second's hesitation and went outside. I turned back to Debbie. "I'm not recording anything. No one will ever know we talked if you don't want them to. Just help me find evidence I can use."

She took a deep breath. "One night, I was working late. I heard people talking in Mr. Rucker's office. Him and the lawyer with the eye patch—we called him Pirate Bob."

I grinned.

"Even Mr. Rucker called him that, but never to his face. But they were in there, and I heard them talking. They said they needed to take control of the situation. That they had to release a statement saying that their medicine had been tampered with. It would be easier to deal with."

"What would be?"

She hesitated. "They knew. The workers there didn't know, but management did. Maybe the board did, too. They knew something was wrong with the medicine, and they made up the Pharma Killer story to cover themselves."

"How did they know? Was it after the boys got sick?"

She nodded. "But that wasn't the first time."

My heart sank. "When was the first time?"

"There were lots of complaints about Herba-Cough Max. Rucker and Pirate Bob buried them. The complaints were never sent to quality control. They just hid them because Herba-Cough was such a big seller. People would call and say the medicine made their kids sick or they thought it had been tampered with or something. We didn't do nothing about it."

"Did they ever mention anything about rat poison?"

She shook her head. "No. I don't know nothing about that. I saw something in the newspaper about it, but I had never heard anything about that. But I know we had hundreds of complaints before they ever put the rat poison out."

"There were hundreds of complaints?"

She nodded. "And that was just in the four years I worked there."

I leaned back into the couch. That was why they had sent me two hundred thousand documents. They weren't trying to hide emails about rat poison; they were hiding all the complaints about Herba-Cough Max. If they'd sent them over at all.

"Debbie, what you signed is known as a contract void from inception. They did something illegal and then had you sign a contract saying you wouldn't tell anybody. That contract is unenforceable, meaning they can't file a suit against you or take any retaliatory action. If they even try, I give you my word that I will take your case, and we will file a counterclaim so huge you will never have to work again. But for now, I need your help."

She looked away, unable to keep eye contact for long.

"They'll do it again, Debbie. If you don't help me, they'll get away with this. They *will* do it again. You don't strike me as the type of person who's just going to sit by and watch that happen."

She chewed on her lower lip. "What would I have to do?"

"First, I need you to write something, and then we have to get it notarized."

# 34

I flew back to Salt Lake with Anto, who fell asleep on the plane ride. He didn't even ask a single question about what Debbie Ochoa and I had talked about or why we had driven her to a bank. The only words we exchanged were when we got to the airport.

He said, "I will send you a bill for my plane ticket."

Debbie Ochoa's affidavit, which was like sworn testimony in writing, had been notarized at the local bank near her house. I held it in a manila envelope. It was too valuable to put in my luggage.

Now, I had to withdraw the lawsuit in state court and refile it in federal court. I would advise Rebecca Whiting to refuse the settlement, regardless of what Marty said. I wanted to shake Pharma-K to its foundations.

Under Utah law, punitive damages were capped at two hundred fifty thousand dollars. Those were the damages meant to punish a company for unethical behavior. So if a corporation killed someone on purpose and buried the body, the most they could be fined in Utah was two hundred fifty thousand. It was no wonder that corporations were moving here in droves.

Luckily, federal courts had no such cap on punitive damages. I had started a damages calculation on the plane: I would be asking for a helluva lot more than we would've gotten in state court. Because Joel had passed, the case had become a wrongful death suit.

First, I had to get Rebecca's approval.

I drove to the hospital, but a nurse told me she had gone home. I called Jessica for the address. Rebecca lived in a section of the city known as Rose Park, in a small white house with a rusted fence. I sat in the driveway for a second, staring at a mitt and baseball bats on the front lawn.

She answered her door right away. Didn't say anything, just hugged me, and led me to the dining table. She seemed different somehow, and I guessed someone at the hospital had given her a sedative. An older woman who vaguely resembled Rebecca nodded to me from the living room, but she didn't say anything.

"I woke up this morning, and I checked his room," she said. "A part of me thought he would be there."

I reached across the table and held her hand. "They've offered two point four million dollars. Our firm is not going to take a cut. I'll convince my partners it's the right thing to do. I'll forward the full amount to you, if you want it."

She swallowed. "Would you take it?"

I hesitated. "No. I would want to make sure this never happened to another kid again. But two million is a lot of money. You could have a completely new life."

"I don't care about my life. They took my life from me. No, I don't want to take anything. I want to make sure no mother has to go through this again because of them."

I nodded and hugged her again. Then I left the house and headed to the law firm.

Marty was sitting at his desk when I walked in. I shut the door and stood in front of him, my arms folded.

"We're not taking the money. I talked to Rebecca. She wants a trial."

Marty shook his head. "Are you an idiot? We could lose a trial. Then where will she be? Huh? She gonna go back to work the next day and be normal?"

"She wants a chance. That's all."

"A chance at what? That's what you don't seem to be understanding: People die all the time. Accidents happen. Cover-ups happen. It fucking happens!"

"It has to be fought."

"We're not Crusaders taking back the Holy Land, Noah. We're personal injury lawyers. We get money for people who are hurt. Joel was hurt, Rebecca was hurt, and we're going to get money for them. That's it. That's all we do."

"That's such bullshit," I said, pointing at him. "You're scared of losing the money we put in."

"Yes, I'm scared. And I'm scared of the cases we're gonna have to turn down while you and half the lawyers here battle this out in court. And by the way, bucko, you were the one who established these rules. I was a divorce lawyer before this firm. You were the one who taught me to never take risks on a case, to always focus on the money and never get attached. These are your rules, and you don't get to break them just because you feel like it!"

"You're a coward. That's the problem."

"Up yours, asshole! I've let you do everything you wanted to do. Have I ever told you not to take a case? Even when I thought it was a dog case, I let you take it, because partners trust each other. But there's no room for trust in Noah Byron's world. He's always right. Whatever he wants, he gets. This one time you didn't get to take a case your way, and you come in here and call me a coward? Up. Yours."

I took a deep breath and sat down in one of the chairs across from him. A headache crept up, and I rubbed my forehead. "They murdered this boy, Marty. What the hell did we go to law school for if we won't even fight people like this?"

Marty put his elbows on the desk. He shook his head, then mumbled something under his breath. It sounded like "Shit."

"Okay," he finally said. "Assuming, just for a second, I go along with you, what would you want us to do?"

"KGB found Debbie Ochoa. She said Bob and Rucker came up with this Pharma Killer thing on their own and leaked it to the press. That they were covering up for medicine that's been causing customer complaints for years. She said she heard them herself, and she's going to testify."

Marty leaned back in the seat. "Holy shit."

"Exactly. Now there's something we gotta do as fast as possible."

# 35

Every employee of the firm came down to the storage unit. We had sent subpoenas for everything Pharma-K had on complaints about Herba-Cough Max, and subpoenas to their Internet service providers, their website developers, and hosting company. Even if Bob and Rucker had deleted the emails from their end, there'd still be records of them from the ISPs.

Between all of them, they had sent over an additional hundred thousand documents.

We hired a couple of temps to answer phone calls. Everyone else came down in jeans, T-shirts, and shorts. We carried the boxes back to the conference rooms and began sorting through them. Boxes filled both conference rooms, then our offices. Then we had to stack them in the hallways of the firm and the lobby. We all went through them—page by page, line by line. I found an email from Rucker calling me a prick.

By afternoon, I had personally read something like five hundred pages. My eyes hurt. We ordered in sandwiches and coffee to keep us awake. Raimi was a machine. He scanned each document with a glance, then moved on to the next one. He easily reviewed triple the pages I did.

"You all right?" I said to him.

He leaned back in the chair of the conference room, blinking a few times to wet his eyes. "I'm fine. I'm surprised Marty went along with this."

"You don't approve?"

"With Debbie Ochoa's testimony, and if we actually find hundreds of complaints like she said . . . I don't know. Too close to call."

I put my hand on his shoulder. "I'm glad you're helping."

"Remember that if we lose and we have to go back to sharing a single office."

We called it a night around one a.m. Olivia and I took three boxes and went to her house. We drank energy drinks and kept going. By four in the morning, we had gone through one of the boxes before we passed out. I slept on her couch and woke up to her mom draping a quilt over me.

"She really likes you, you know," she whispered. "She doesn't normally fall this hard."

I watched her leave the room and looked around to find Olivia on the love seat, snoring. I grinned as I turned away and fell back to sleep.

The next day, sometime around two in the afternoon, Raimi found the first complaint from a customer. A mother had emailed to complain that her six-year-old had started vomiting after taking Herba-Cough Max. From there, the complaints kept coming. Bob's lackeys had spread the complaints over several boxes rather than stacking them with each other, no doubt hoping we wouldn't see how many there really were.

By six in the afternoon, 254 complaints lay on one of the conference tables. All from parents, all delineating the same symptoms: confusion, vomiting, sleepiness, fatigue, inability to expend energy, migraines, and blood in the stool or vomit. All of them had received the same reply email:

*We're sorry you're unhappy with your product. Please return the unused portion to us, and a full refund will be issued.*

Pharma-K wanted the unused portion returned—it couldn't be tested that way.

I couldn't help but wonder why no one had died in the four years the complaints had been racking up. Of the hundreds of children made sick by this medicine, why did Joel die and everyone else live?

"Raimi," I said calmly, staring at the documents, "will you please draft a new complaint for federal court? I want one million in actual damages, and a hundred fifty million in punitive damages for the death of Joel Whiting."

# 36

I had never met another attorney who was as good at document drafting as Raimi was. He drafted the new complaint in one day, and we withdrew the suit in state court. We sent the new complaint to Bob, who called me, swearing and screaming before the phone was even up to my ear. The call only ended when he threw his phone, and it must've broken.

Federal court was a different ball game than state court, though the rules were similar. Juries received better instructions; the judges were smarter and didn't tolerate any nonsense. Any frivolous tactic would receive a verbal reprimand, and if it happened again, sanctions would follow.

At the first hearing, Bob handed me a revised 12(b)(6) motion. I gave it to Raimi, who had the reply ready in two days. This time, we attached Debbie Ochoa's affidavit and the 254 complaints. The judge didn't even hold a hearing. He denied the defense's motion and set a trial date.

More depositions followed, along with more requests for documents and more interrogatories. These weren't the blanket depositions

I'd ordered earlier: we chose only those employees who would know about the Herba-Cough complaints and why they hadn't been acted upon. Debbie helped us narrow down the list to twenty people.

The federal courts weren't nearly as busy as the state courts were, so the case moved along swiftly.

This case was what was called a "battle of the experts." On our side, we had two pharmacists, two chemists, and two toxicologists. They had all agreed on the theory that cyanide poisoning, which had damaged his kidneys and liver beyond repair, had caused Joel Whiting's death, and that the poison was contained in Pharma-K's product, which—after a court order to the police department and the Utah State Crime Lab— we had independently tested twice. Both tests confirmed the presence not of cyanide itself but of acetonitrile. If swallowed, acetonitrile metabolized to cyanide in the body.

I had sent KGB out to talk to every former employee we could find. We located a former Pharma-K chemist who'd worked in their labs. KGB found him in New Jersey, working for a different company. He was going to come testify that the company had manufactured nail polish remover that contained acetonitrile. Our expert affirmed that the Utah location was the only plant that had produced the polish remover. He suspected that the acetonitrile had gotten into the Herba-Cough Max in small doses.

"You're sure about that?" I asked him on the phone.

"Not to a certainty, no. The rat poison brand that was used contained acetonitrile and could certainly cause death, but it's highly doubtful. The complaints go back four years, so it seems unlikely that rat poison would be getting into the medicine for that long. I suspect it's the nail polish remover."

"They seemed pretty concerned about the rat poison."

"They probably don't know how the poison got into their medicine and were scared. If I were a betting man, though, it's the nail polish remover."

"Why would these three cases be worse than the ones four years ago? Why would Joel Whiting be the only death?"

"That I don't know. Maybe whatever flaw in the procedure they have has gotten worse and more of the acetonitrile is getting into the product. It's tough to say. What I can say is that the nail polish remover made in that plant definitely contains the same chemical that boy died of."

We had our link.

But on the other side, the defense had two chemists, two toxicologists, and two pharmacists. They had matched us, expert for expert.

Olivia and I worked every angle. We conducted depositions together where she would ask questions I didn't even think of. She focused on details in a way I never could. If a witness being deposed mentioned a date, she knew just from reading the file what day it was and what the weather was like. I never would've remembered that stuff in a million years. She caught one witness saying he was working on a February eleventh, a Sunday, the day the plant was closed, and he quickly had to take back everything he'd said. Throwing his entire testimony into doubt.

She took the Bar sometime between depositions, and received her letter informing her she passed a couple of months later. I knew only because I'd heard one of our other clerks talking about it. Olivia didn't even bring it up.

"We need to celebrate," I said.

I took her out that night to a restaurant on the top floor of a building overlooking downtown Salt Lake. We sat at a table by the windows; I ordered the most expensive bottle of wine they had, and I drank it while Olivia sipped at a diet cola. Before the meal came out, she held my hand.

I smiled and sipped at my wine. "How about we talk about how you just passed the Bar?"

"It's nothing. Eighty percent of my class passed it."

"It's something. Marty failed it his first time."

"Get out."

"See? I can tell by the way you reacted that it does matter. Don't be modest; this is a big deal. You're going to be able to sue people and subpoena them. It's a powerful gift the government's giving you. I was hoping that since you know you have the choice now, you wouldn't go into the nonprofit realm."

"I still want to. In some capacity at least. Why are you against it?"

"I don't like the fake righteousness of it. Like they're somehow doing something pure. They're seeking profit, just like every other cutthroat business out there. But it's worse because they're not honest about it."

"Maybe. Or maybe I'll help make the one I work at better. Have it be an example to other nonprofits."

We ate and talked for over two hours. The night sky sparkled through the glass, and Salt Lake lit up in a display of yellows, reds, and blues. The Walker Center, a skyscraper with a tower on top that changed color according to the weather, had turned a light red, indicating more heat tomorrow.

At the car, after coming down from the restaurant, we held each other and kissed.

In the morning, she came over and made us breakfast. I sat at the table and read the newspaper on my iPad. Having someone else there, treating my home like her own, was something I had missed but had never admitted to myself that I had.

We ate together before heading out to the Hyatt. I had rented their best conference room and ordered expensive pastries. Marty had set up another settlement negotiation.

This time, we came in force. Raimi and Marty sat at the ends of the table, Olivia sat next to me, and every associate at our firm was there. Bob came with the intent to intimidate, as well. He brought Rucker and at least twenty lawyers, and the hotel had to bring in more chairs. No one touched the food. No one talked. The defense attorneys weren't sneering at me or whispering to themselves. This time, they were scared of losing a big client and maybe hurting their reputation in the process. Not just that, but they understood that I knew someone had advised Pharma-K to break the law and lie about a serial killer poisoning their medicine. The Bar and the FBI would both be watching the outcome of this case.

"Hello again, Bob."

His upper lip curled, and he pushed a tablet to me. Figures were filled in on a spreadsheet. The bottom total was $4,150,658.98. The ninety-eight cents was my favorite part.

"Four point one," Bob said. "She'll be a rich woman."

"Not enough."

"How is that not enough? It's one child."

"I saw the emails, Bob. It's not just one child—it's hundreds. See, I think what you're really scared of is that I'm going to contact all of them and put them together for a class action against Pharma-K. Then I'm not asking for a hundred fifty million. I'm asking for a billion. Does Pharma-K have a billion dollars on hand to pay those suits, Bob?"

"You're in over your head. I will bury you. I'll drag this out so long your firm will go under before you can fucking say one word to a jury."

Rucker put a hand on Bob's arm. "Bob, that's enough." He looked at me. "Six million dollars. And another two million each for the other two kids who got sick, if their lawyers will take it. That's ten million spread to three kids. Ten million is what you wanted at some point. It was pie in the sky, a negotiating starting point that you knew would get cut down over time. But I'm willing to give it to you."

I hesitated, seeing that Marty was practically licking his lips. "Not good enough," I said.

"Then what the hell is good enough?" Rucker said, anger in his voice.

"I want this plant closed. I want everybody responsible for this fired. I want full disclosure to the public and the FDA. I want the FDA to inspect everything, full access, and figure out how this happened. Then I want four million for Rebecca Whiting, and I want another four million to set up a nonprofit in Joel Whiting's name. Its mission will be consumer protection. And I want all of the people that complained about the medicine reimbursed for any expenses."

The lawyers on the other side laughed.

"You're talking about a loss of easily fifty million from closing the plant," Bob said. "If we litigate this and lose, no matter what you ask for, the jury might—*might*—award Rebecca Whiting a million, maybe less. There is no way we're agreeing to those terms."

"Then we're done here." I stood up. "Enjoy the pastries. They're delicious."

# 37

Over the next several months, Bob, true to his word, made my life miserable. He filed motion after motion after motion. I had to draft a response to each one he filed. And then there would be a hearing and oral arguments on the motion. Sometimes, the judge would want additional briefing after that and then additional arguments. Some of the motions were good. Bob filed a motion in limine—a motion filed before trial that dealt with something improper that hadn't been brought up before—asking to exclude Rebecca Whiting's testimony based on Rule 403 in the Federal Rules of Evidence, the rule governing when evidence was relevant but too prejudicial to be presented to a jury.

He made an eloquent argument as to why the jury would be so swayed by her testimony that they would disregard any facts contrary to whatever Rebecca Whiting said. Even Judge Dustin Hoss, an older man with red hair, was impressed and said so on the record. The motion was denied, of course, but it showed what kind of work Walcott could produce if he wanted to.

Most of the motions weren't like that. Most of them were garbage meant to drain us. Bob knew my firm had devoted most of our resources to this case and that we'd had to start turning away other cases. He just had to conduct a war of attrition and drag it out as long as he possibly could. Our firm would eventually run out of money, and we would have to settle or dismiss the case.

Our only saving grace was that we were in federal court. When I informed the judge that I had received three hundred thousand documents, he forced Walcott to catalogue every document and create a searchable index for me. By that point, we'd already done that, but it was still nice to see Bob ordered to do something he didn't want to do.

After the eleventh motion filed, Judge Hoss had finally had enough. He demanded that Walcott write one motion containing the various claims, defenses, counterclaims, and motions in limine the defense wanted to present. Bob objected, but the judge was fed up and wanted this case before a jury.

Olivia worked eighteen hours a day for a week straight, leaving only to check on her mother and make sure she ate and took her medications, in order to get a jump on a reply motion to the final motion Bob was supposed to file. Raimi was supervising her work and told me one day, out of the blue, "We need to keep her at all costs. Her motions are amazing."

Bob never filed his motion. My guess was that, though Walcott had resources, Pharma-K didn't want to be their treasure chest indefinitely. At some point, the company had gotten a fat bill from Walcott, and someone had been yelled at. The trial was set, and Bob informed the judge at the pretrial conference that he was prepared to go forward.

---

Olivia had her swearing-in ceremony. I was the only one there for her. I held her for a long time afterward, as tears streamed down her cheeks.

We ate lunch at a seafood restaurant and talked about the ACLU. Now that she was officially a member of the Utah Bar, she had been offered a position there through a high school friend. She'd informed them that she would come work for them as soon as the Joel Whiting case was over.

Olivia spent some nights at my house, but only after checking on her mom and making sure she took her medication. Some nights, I slept at her house on the couch. It was uncomfortable as all hell, but I knew Olivia didn't like sleeping away from her mother without someone there to watch after her.

Sex was frequently on my mind. Olivia had a beauty to her that was so natural, I'm not even sure she understood how appealing she was to men. She wasn't the type to be on the cover of a magazine; she was the type you wanted to wake up next to every morning.

Sex, though, to her, was strictly something that occurred during a marriage. Six months ago, that would've been the death knell in our relationship. Now, it seemed like a minor thing. I enjoyed being around her more than anyone else in my life. In many ways, she was smarter than I was and challenged everything I thought about the world and myself. It seemed like, every day, she took time to make sure I understood how lucky I was and felt gratitude about the position I was in. Slowly, I noticed that my mood began to improve. Most mornings I woke up late and only grudgingly, but I was starting to get up earlier and with purpose. She was making me a better person.

One night, we sat on my balcony and watched the full moon. A gorgeous white bulb in an ink-black sky.

"Raimi said you write the best motions he's ever seen," I told her. "He said we need to offer you whatever salary you need to stay."

"You once told me not to become a lawyer. Now you want to make me rich to be one?"

I shrugged. "Maybe it just took some time for me to realize it's not all bad."

That was partly true. The other part was that I liked seeing her every day. I liked walking into the office and seeing her in a conference room.

The way she would smile at me. Her hair falling onto her shoulders, her slender fingers busy working on a MacBook, her eyes that lit up when she saw me. I didn't want to share her with anyone else. I wanted her completely and utterly to myself.

---

The trial was approaching, and I hadn't been out to visit Rebecca in a few months. It was a couple of days after the first day of winter, and snow coated the city. Snow had a way of silencing everything, and the city just seemed quiet. I stood outside her home a few moments and enjoyed the silence before knocking.

She answered. She looked much skinnier. Her hair was different, and she was wearing glasses.

"Sorry to just pop in."

"No, you can come over anytime."

We sat on the couch, and she offered me tea. She seemed more with it, though I could tell she was still on some sort of medication that slowed her movements, her speech, and her train of thought.

"The trial's next week, and I think we're as prepared as we can be. It's going to start with jury selection, but you'll have to be there for that since you're the plaintiff."

"We only went through my testimony a couple of times. Do you want to do it more?"

I shook my head. "No. I want it from the heart, not from memory."

"I remember your wedding," she said. "You looked so handsome. I told Tia that you were the handsomest man I had ever seen. She blushed and told me she thought that, too. I wished you two could've made it."

"It worked out for the best. I think we're both happier now, and it wouldn't have happened if we stuck it out."

Rebecca seemed to zone out for a moment, her eyes glazing over as she scanned the room. As though she didn't remember where she was.

"Rebecca, do you have any questions about court for me?"

She asked a few questions about where the court was and what time she should be there. Then she asked the same questions again. She would ask a single question several times in a row. It was clear the medication she was on was affecting her ability to think.

"Excuse me a second." I walked outside to the front porch and called Olivia. Within twenty minutes, she was sitting on the couch next to Rebecca and holding her hand.

"Do you remember me?" she asked.

"Of course. You were very nice to me and my son. I appreciated that."

"Rebecca, what medications are you on?"

"Why, dear?"

"Noah and I just want to make sure you're okay."

She looked toward the kitchen. "They're all right there. You can see for yourself. I don't know their names."

I followed Olivia into the kitchen as she lifted each amber bottle and looked at the names. One of her legs crossed behind the other and for a moment, I felt bad about yanking her into this. She'd seen enough heartache with her own mother. I leaned against the kitchen counter, my arms folded.

"It's the amcipetyline," she said. "My mom's on that. It saps energy levels. Almost like a sedative."

"She can't testify like this. Bob will tear her apart on the stand. We need to push the trial back."

"Can we do that?"

"I don't know. Federal trial set for eight weeks . . . I don't know."

"Let me talk to her doctor. There's another medication that's just as effective but doesn't have the same side effects."

I waited outside while Olivia and Rebecca made the calls. A ball of anxiety rolled around in my gut. I could see my frosty breath in the air and it was, somehow, exhilarating. Proof that I was alive and fighting. Not just some drone stuck in an office reading documents ten hours a day.

The door finally opened and Olivia stepped out. She shut it behind her.

"We've talked to the doctor and they're going to switch her to Lexapro."

"Is that, I mean, I don't want to put her in harm's way just for—"

"No, it's perfectly safe. As safe as the medication she was on anyway. She wants to do it. She doesn't want this to ever happen to anyone again. She's a really tough lady, Noah. She'll go on. It won't be easy, and she won't be the same, but she'll go on."

I exhaled loudly and watched Rebecca through the window in the front room. She sat on the couch and stared at the television, though it wasn't on. I had seen my own father do that. A gaze that held no meaning and expected nothing from the world.

"Thank you for this," I said to Olivia. "For all of it. For everything."

"You don't have to thank me. Just kick Bob's ass."

I had a few hours, so I went to the courthouse. I found it open and sat inside, staring up at the judge's bench and the jury box close to the plaintiff's table. Six jurors would be assigned to this case. Jury selection on a case worth this much could go fast, or it could take weeks. You never knew until you had the jury pool right in front of you. Jury consultants would be hired, the potential jurors' social media posts analyzed, friends and neighbors interviewed. I wasn't involved in any of it. We'd found a long time ago that Marty was masterful at analyzing a potential juror's background information and personal history and predicting the likelihood that he or she would find for our plaintiff. He would spearhead the jury selection, but in the meantime, he'd be unable to work his cases or take any new ones. I'd learned from our accountant that we had one and a half million cash on hand. If we didn't bring in any other payments, but stopped our advertising, that would last us nine months. After that, we would be bankrupt.

I rose and stood over the jury box, staring at the seats the men and women who would decide my fate and the fate of my firm would sit in.

I ran my hand along the banister. I sat in one of the seats and tried to picture what the jurors were going to see, to hear what they were going to hear. I could do neither, so I got up and left.

That night, I lay with Olivia in her bed, and we watched television—something I never did at night because I knew the blue light interfered with sleep. Now I welcomed the background noise.

"Are you scared?" she asked.

"Yes."

"Why?"

"Because if I fail, I'm not sure we can bounce back. We've spent so much money that we need a big win. All those people are relying on me, and I feel like I don't really know what I'm doing."

She took my face gently in her hands. "I'm proud of you."

We turned off the television, and I fell asleep in her arms.

# 38

Voir dire, jury selection, came and went at about the pace I anticipated. During voir dire, we could exclude jurors we thought were prejudicial to our case. Marty had excluded fifty percent of the pool, and Bob— or more accurately, Bob's jury-consulting firm—had excluded another twenty-five percent. That left us with the six men and women and two alternates who would hear the trial. The entire process took two weeks.

Bob had used the standard tricks: trying to question the potential jurors in a way that would taint the case. Instead of saying, "Can you be fair in a case involving an injured child?" he would ask, "If you found an injured child's mother was forcing the child to fake injuries, could you still be impartial?" It was all obvious and devious, and I hoped the jury saw through it.

During those two weeks, I practiced cross-examination and brushed up on the Rules of Evidence, hoping to impress the jury by not having to look anything up. Lawyers on television knew every relevant rule by heart, but the law was about the gray area in between the rule and what the drafters of the rule meant. There was too much information to memorize, but I hoped I could minimize the number of times the trial paused while the lawyers and the judge had to research and argue something.

The first day of trial came without fanfare.

I got out of bed, showered, and shaved like I would on any other day. I chose a suit, but not one of my more expensive ones. I clipped a San Francisco Giants pin to my lapel.

Olivia and I would be trying the case together. Raimi had severe social anxiety around strangers and couldn't say a word in courtrooms, and Marty was nearly the same. He had lost forty divorce cases in a row when I had found him. But he knew how to make people feel good when they signed up with him. That was a skill no one talked about in law school, but that was invaluable to a lawyer.

On the day of opening statements, I sat down and flipped through the jury instructions. I hadn't even read them; Raimi had prepared them. Then they'd been perfected through a long process of passing them back and forth between the plaintiff and defense counsel, making corrections until there were no more corrections to be made.

Bob had five lawyers there with him and, most disturbingly, wasn't wearing his eye patch. He had taken it off before voir dire and his eye was completely fine. Seeing both of them exposed was somehow disconcerting.

Rebecca Whiting sat next to me. This was her lawsuit now, for the loss of her son. Olivia sat on my other side. I'd discovered throughout the depositions that she was a pit bull at cross-examination. When a lawyer was too aggressive with a witness, the jury had a tendency to turn against them. To view them as a bully. But some witnesses required it. I would use her for that, so that the jury still got the information but associated the aggression with her instead of me. She was thrilled at the idea that she would get up in court and yell at people who'd hurt children and covered it up, and they wouldn't be able to do anything in turn.

We sat up straight as the jury was called out.

Judge Hoss reviewed the preliminary instructions. He had a dry, boring manner of speaking, as though he were reading a cereal box. But it was good because it contrasted so well with how I spoke that I hoped it would make the jury pay more attention to what I was saying.

"Counsel, the time is now yours for opening statement."

I looked at the jury. I didn't know their names or what they liked and didn't like. I trusted that Raimi and Marty knew me and had picked a jury that would respond to what I had to say. I took out my phone and looked at a photo underneath the table so the jury couldn't see. It was the one taken of Joel at the hospital when he was making a silly face. I stared at it for a few seconds, then placed my phone on the chair before rising and standing in front of them.

"My father . . . was an alcoholic. My earliest memory of him is him standing on the table of a restaurant, drunk and cursing out the wait-ress that was trying to get him down. My mother sat at the end of the table and didn't say anything. She was a strong woman, but there was only so much she could take. She left us when I was young. I didn't understand either of my parents. What that thing was inside my father that made him drink and grow brutally violent, or what that thing was inside my mother that caused her to leave her only son in his hands. My entire life I've tried to understand it, and sometimes I still feel like that boy huddled underneath his bed, hoping the footsteps would keep going past his room.

"My father was a monster, but he was an honest monster. He never hid what he was. But there are worse monsters in the world. There are monsters that hide themselves in broad daylight. Monsters that put on smiles, that might even shake your hand and call you their friend. There are monsters in this world that care nothing about goodness, or people, or the future. We used to search under our beds for monsters when we were young, but that's not where they were. They were out in the open, pretending to be there to help us." I pointed to the table with Bob and his lawyers. "Pharma-K is one of these monsters."

I walked over and stood in between the defense and plaintiff tables. "This is Rebecca Whiting. She is the plaintiff. She is flesh and bone. Her son was killed by medicine manufactured by Pharma-K. But look at the defense table. This woman and all these men are lawyers. Where is Pharma-K? Where is the person to hold responsible for the death of Joel Whiting? He doesn't exist. He's only on paper. He is a monster that hides behind money and laws."

I put my hands in my pockets and came back in front of the jurors.

"Most people think our system allows the little guy to rise. Like Oscar Wilde said, the poor in America don't think of themselves as a repressed lower class, but as temporarily embarrassed millionaires. We're told that every person in the world has magic in them—the ability to pursue what they love and make something of themselves. That's the freedom that's been promised to us since the day we were born . . . but something's not right.

"I've seen it firsthand. I've been watching something happen since I was a kid. It's so subtle that most people don't even see it. They don't realize it's happening . . . we're not free anymore.

"The most powerful corporations and banks hire the most expensive lobbyists, who buy the votes of the most powerful politicians. Capitalism is a free exchange between two entities without the use of force. That's not what we have anymore. The word for what we have is *oligarchy.* It means that we are ruled by a few powerful people. Our system is rigged, and the people who benefit are the richest corporations. The White House and Congress are our symbols of freedom and leadership, but that's all they are: symbols. The richest corporations lead us.

"Pharma-K is also one of these corporations. They hurt people over and over again, and they cover it up. Why? Because they can. They know that our system isn't set up to go after them. Our system, our entire system, is set up to protect them."

I paused.

"Joel Whiting was twelve years old when his mother gave him an ordinary dose of Herba-Cough Max cough suppressant. Within an hour, he was at the hospital with cyanide poisoning. Along with two other boys from Salt Lake County. He fought—he fought damn hard—but the cyanide had damaged his kidneys and liver to the point that there wasn't any hope left for him. He passed away two and a half months after taking that dose of Herba-Cough Max. A drug that I will show you had racked up two hundred fifty-four complaints and was still not removed from the market. A drug that this company knew was dangerous.

"We will have Dr. Cornelius Pier testify that he used to work for Pharma-K as their lead chemist. They tried to get into the cosmetics market, and they produced a nail polish remover that they advertised as 'the most powerful nail polish remover in history.' The nail polish remover contained a chemical called acetonitrile. The doctor will testify to you that acetonitrile turns into cyanide in the body if it's swallowed. For four years, that nail polish remover somehow got into their children's medicine, and they did everything in their power to cover it up, including fabricating a story about a serial killer poisoning children's medicine."

I looked at Rebecca, who held my gaze.

"Everything Joel ever was and everything he could've been was wiped away by this company. He will never graduate high school, he will never know what it feels like to kiss a girl, he will never hit a home run on his baseball team, never get married, never know the feeling of seeing his child born, and never grow old and watch the world change. Everything he had was taken from him"—I pointed to the defense table—"because that company thought they could save a few bucks by not recalling the medicine."

I stepped close to the jury.

"We're told by this system that you are the car you drive or the size of your house or the number in your bank account. We're taught from an early age by advertising agencies that we're only as good as the wealth we have. It isn't true. We're not their slaves. We're people. We're not numbers on a spreadsheet. We aren't disposable if we don't make enough. This is our country, not theirs.

"If you want a description of what they are, they're murderers. They murdered that boy as surely as if they'd put a bullet in him. This isn't about money. This isn't about winning. This is about a little boy who was an inconvenient cell on a spreadsheet, and they didn't care what happened to him.

"Joel Whiting"—I glanced at Olivia, then looked back at the jury— "was my friend. Don't let him die in vain."

I sat down. Bob stood up and buttoned the top button of his suit coat. He walked in front of the jury and put his hands behind his back, like a professor about to lecture. "The story of the pharmaceutical industry in this country is a story of saving lives. Companies like Pharma-K are responsible for preventing the deaths and improving the lives of countless people throughout the world. And they dare call us murderers? *Murderers?* Pharma-K did everything they could when they found out someone had poisoned their medicine. And that is what happened, contrary to anything the plaintiff's lawyers will tell you. Someone tampered with the medicine and killed that boy. I won't begin to tell you I understand it. I don't think anyone can understand it. The FBI constructed a psychological profile on the man who did this, and we'll introduce that to you so you can get a better sense of the type of evil responsible for this, but don't let the plaintiff's lawyers fool you. This *is* about money. It is always about money with them.

"They're asking you for a total of one hundred fifty-one million dollars. For what? Because the product was tampered with? It had a seal. When the CEO of Pharma-K found out about the poisonings, he set up a task force that met twice a day to investigate what happened and pull the tainted medicine from the shelves. He is a father, too. He has children. He knows what it would feel like to lose a child, and he no more wanted this to happen than you did. But that's life, isn't it? We take our chances. Every time you get on the road, you're taking a chance that some psychotic isn't driving one of the two-ton steel machines barreling toward you and isn't just going to swerve into your lane. You take your chances that a drunk driver isn't going to come out of nowhere and slam into you. When you get on a plane, you take your chances that it won't crash, that terrorists won't hijack it, that there won't be someone with a contagious illness sharing the same air as you. You take your chances.

"Sometimes, in this life, people lose. I wish, and I know everyone at Pharma-K wishes, that we could bring Joel Whiting back, but we can't. Even if his mother got the millions of dollars she was asking for, it wouldn't bring him back. He's gone. An evil that few of us can understand took him from us. I wish I could bring him back, ladies and gentlemen, but I can't. All I can do is stand here and tell you that this company, one started by a father and son, cares about its customers. It cares about the people who take its medicine. It is a company devoted to healing, not destroying. Their pride and joy right now is a pain medication that will not cause addiction. Can you imagine the benefits to those people who suffer every day with chronic pain? On the horizon is a drug that will treat patients living with AIDS for one-twentieth the cost of the current medications. Pharma-K is trying to change the world for the better. They are not murderers. There is no basis for this lawsuit other than the pain the plaintiff feels."

He turned to Rebecca. "I'm sorry, Ms. Whiting. I truly am. But putting this company out of business, a company that tried to save your son, isn't the answer."

He sat back down.

The judge looked at me and said, "First witness, Mr. Byron."

# 39

Rebecca was my first witness. She rose slowly and walked up to the witness stand. The clerk swore her in, and when she was settled, I stood before her. I asked the preliminary required questions to establish her identity. Then I said, "Tell us what happened on April seventh of this year."

She swallowed. "Joel hadn't been feeling well. He had a cough that just wouldn't go away. I ran to the store and got him some cough medicine." She paused. "I just chose the most expensive one. When it came to Joel's health . . ." She didn't say anything for a good half minute after that as she fought back tears. "I chose that medicine, and I took it home. Joel was outside, playing. He loved baseball. That was his favorite thing in the world. He came inside, so I gave him some medicine, just the dose it said on the bottle, and he went into the living room. I didn't hear him, though. I thought it was strange. So I went out to check on him, and that's when I found him. He was unconscious, and vomit was everywhere."

"What did you do?"

"I called an ambulance. They came and took us to the hospital. At first, they told me it was a stroke. And then they thought it was a heart attack. And then they didn't know what it was, not until a nurse said that she had seen on the news that another little boy got sick from taking some children's medicine. So she asked me if I had given him any Herba-Cough Max." Tears appeared in her eyes and rolled down her cheeks. "I felt like I was going to die when she asked me that. Just the look on her face, and I knew it was something awful."

"What did the nurse do?"

"She was nice enough to run to my house and get the medicine. They brought it back and tested it, and it tested positive for that thing you said. Acetonitrile."

"What happened to Joel?"

"He lived for almost three months. He fought hard. As hard as a little boy could fight. But too much damage had been done. They said they wouldn't give him a kidney transplant because he was too sick. So he died on July second." She wiped tears from her cheeks but wasn't sobbing. "He fought until the last minute. You can't imagine the pain he went through. Toward the end, some nights he'd be screaming, and the pain medication just couldn't touch it. So I'd sit with him and hold him all night."

I waited for a moment, pretending to stare at my notes. I felt the tears welling up, and I had to close my eyes for a few seconds before I could open them again. "Did you ever try to get in touch with Pharma-K?"

"Yes. I tried and tried. No one would talk to me. Not until Debbie Ochoa. She was one of their secretaries. She told me that—"

"Objection. Hearsay," Bob said.

"Goes to state of mind, Judge," I replied. "I'm not arguing as to its truth, just that it was stated to my client. And Ms. Ochoa will be testifying to verify any statements made."

"I'll allow it."

I turned to Rebecca. "What did Debbie Ochoa say?"

"She said that they had known about the medicine making children sick for years. That they covered it up. That they were the ones that announced this serial killer story so they wouldn't have to pay claims. I was so relieved someone was talking to me from there. But then a couple of weeks after, she was fired, and I never heard from her again."

"Did anyone else talk to you?"

"No. At one point, one of the managers told me to piss off. He said Joel was one customer and that they had bigger things to worry about. That's when I started asking my friends if they knew a lawyer. And God sent us you, Mr. Byron."

I looked down to the floor for a second, then went to the jury and leaned on the banister in front of them. "Why did you file this lawsuit, Rebecca?"

"I just want to make sure this doesn't happen to anyone else's child. That's all. They wouldn't even talk to me. They didn't care that a little boy was dying from their product. I can't just sit by and watch them hurt more people. It has nothing to do with the money."

"You said it has nothing to do with the money, but we're asking them for millions of dollars."

"I would give it all up for one minute with Joel again. Just to hug him and tell him I love him. But they can't do that. The law can't give me back my boy and it won't put these people in jail. It won't do anything but say that I can ask for money. That's the only justice Joel gets."

I nodded. "Nothing further."

Bob stood up and moved uncomfortably close to Rebecca. "You said you just want to make sure that this doesn't happen again, but that's not true, is it?"

"It is."

"You had our attention months ago. If all you wanted was better safety procedures, the company would've listened."

"I tried. I tried to talk to anyone over there, and no one would talk to me."

"So you filed a lawsuit for a hundred and fifty-one million dollars? This is about money, Ms. Whiting."

"I don't want your blood money. I'm going to give it all away."

Bob hadn't expected her to say that, and he took a second before continuing. "Tell us about Joel's illness."

"What illness?"

"Ms. Whiting," he said, "are you going to sit in front of this jury and pretend that you don't know what I'm talking about?" He pulled out several sheets of paper and showed them to me before heading to the witness box. They contained Joel's medical history. I'd known this was coming at some point in the trial, and just had to let it happen and hope I could repair the damage later. I'd prepared Rebecca as best I could, and she seemed confident on the stand. A reserved, justified anger emanated from her furious glances toward the defense table.

"Approach, Judge?" he said.

"Certainly."

He went over to Rebecca. "What is this?"

"Medical records."

"And what is the name on the top of these medical records?"

"Joel Whiting."

"I would direct your attention to the entry for September of 2013. Please flip there and read what it says."

She read the page silently first. "No, this was just a conjecture. He wasn't diagnosed."

"Please read it."

"Patient displays abnormal white cell count."

"Abnormal. And what exactly was abnormal about it?"

"They were too low."

"Why did the doctor think it was too low?"

She glanced toward me. "They thought Joel might've had lupus. But he was never officially diagnosed."

"Lupus is an immune disorder, isn't it? Making him more susceptible to anything in the environment that his body would have to fight off."

"He didn't have it."

"But you don't know, do you? You don't know because you never went back to the doctor."

"He didn't have it. They told me it could just be his normal count."

"And then they scheduled a follow-up. One you never showed up for?" He stepped closer to her. "Don't you think the doctors, after Joel's poisoning, could've done more if they'd known he might've had lupus? If you had gone back and gotten him an official diagnosis, maybe they could've done more."

She shook her head. Bob's entire strategy was to blame her for her own son's death, to make her feel responsible. Despite my preparation, it was working. Rebecca was now sobbing, the tears streaming down her cheeks.

Bob was right: lupus could explain why the other hundreds of children lived and Joel didn't. But under the law, it didn't matter if Joel had it or not, because of something called the "eggshell skull doctrine." Someone who hurt someone else took them as they came: if they were diseased or injured, the defendant was responsible for all the injuries, even if they wouldn't have happened if the plaintiff were well. Though legally we were on solid ground, a jury might be put off by the fact that Rebecca never followed up on a potentially fatal diagnosis.

"No. I don't know. I didn't want him to have that diagnosis. He was so young. I didn't want him scared."

Bob looked at the jury and then sat back down with a grin on his face.

# 40

The next six witnesses were our experts. Expert witness cross-examination was the same for both sides: we tried to poke holes in their motivations. The first question any good lawyer asked was "How much were you paid by opposing counsel to be here?" It instantly threw their entire testimony into question. Bob did it masterfully on each witness, everyone except Dr. Pier.

Pier had quit Pharma-K and had nothing to gain by being at the trial, so Bob tried to make him seem like a jaded former employee. At one point, Bob said, "And you're ticked off, aren't you? You're upset that you quit this start-up company and that they are a success now and you missed your lottery ticket?"

Pier shook his head. "Absolutely not. I left because I didn't feel they were following best practices for the industry."

"I have here an email from you, sent in August of the year you quit, to another employee of Pharma-K. Would you please read it for the jury?"

Pier looked at it, and his jaw muscles clenched. He then read it. "It says, 'I'm sick of this bullshit pay. I'm easily worth three times what they're paying. I'll be jumping ship.'"

"'Jumping ship'? Those were your exact words, weren't they?"

"Yes."

"Again, this was about money, wasn't it? It had nothing to do with best practices."

"The money was a factor, but it wasn't the only factor."

"But just a second ago, you said that it was because of best practices. You didn't mention anything about money to this jury. And now when confronted with the truth, you're changing your testimony?"

Pier flushed a rosy color but didn't say anything else.

"That's what I thought," Bob said, moving away from the witness stand.

I leaned over to Olivia and whispered, "How'd we miss that email?"

"Someone must've read it and didn't think it was important."

Our experts' testimonies lasted fourteen entire days. One day, Bob did nothing but object to every question. I would ask someone their name, and Bob would object. He looked like a jerk in front of the jury, but he also threw me off my game because I kept having to ask the same question over again. I lost my rhythm, and sometimes, I had to cut my examination short.

One night, Olivia and I lay on beach chairs on my balcony and sipped virgin margaritas. We were so exhausted, we fell asleep out there and only woke up when my neighbor Jim got into a fight with his girlfriend and the cops were called. I went over there and spoke to the police. They decided to let Jim off with a citation for disorderly conduct, and I told him I would take care of it. The next morning, I had to ask Olivia if I'd dreamed it or if it had really happened.

After the experts, we had Debbie Ochoa flown out, and she was staying in the best hotel we could get. She arrived in the courtroom dressed in a red dress with heels, and I noticed some of the male jurors following her with their eyes. She took the stand and was sworn in.

"What's your name, ma'am?"

"Debra Lucy Ochoa."

"And what is your connection to this case?" I asked.

"I was a secretary at Pharma-K Pharmaceuticals."

"How long did you work there?"

"From 2010 to 2014."

"Do you recall a conversation with Rebecca Whiting, my client, after the news broke about the children who had gotten sick from Herba-Cough Max?"

"Yes. She would call every day. She wanted to know what had happened to her son. We'd been told not to speak to anyone about the cases, but she started crying on the phone one day, and I felt bad. So I told her about what happened."

"And what did you say?"

"I had heard Mr. Rucker talking about the poisonings with Pirate Bo—with the lawyer there."

Bob's face flushed a light pink and he looked behind him at Rucker, who shrugged innocently.

"It was late, and they didn't think I was still there," Debbie continued. "They kept saying that they needed to contain this. That the liability would be huge, and they needed to find a way to get blame off Pharma-K. That's how they came up with the serial killer."

"They came up with it?"

"Yes. I think it was the lawyer. He said that they should issue a press release now, before it became big news. That they should set up a task force and do everything they could to find the person who did this. But there was no person. They made it all up."

I observed with satisfaction as one of the female jurors gave Bob a nasty glare.

"And you heard this yourself?"

"Yes. When they were done speaking, they came out of the office and were surprised that I was there. They didn't think anybody was. I had to work late that night. A week later, they asked for me to resign."

"Who asked?"

"My direct boss, James Olsen. He said that I was a good employee but that Rucker wanted another secretary, so he said he was going to give me twenty-five thousand dollars as a severance package, and if I wanted, the company had a condo in California that I could live in for free."

"For free?"

"Yes. No rent. So I didn't go to HR or anything. Free rent and twenty-five grand is a lot for me."

"Were you aware, Ms. Ochoa, of any complaints to the company about Herba-Cough Max?"

She nodded. "Yes. Hundreds of them. I was the secretary for the consumer affairs division. Parents would call me all the time about it. They said it made their children sick. I would tell Mr. Olsen and Mr. Rucker, but they said that it was a quality-control issue. They wouldn't do anything."

"In the four years you worked there, how many complaints would you say you got?"

"I don't know. Maybe six or seven hundred total calls. A few hundred emails."

I had subpoenaed call logs and recordings, and the company had responded that such records were kept for only thirty days and then destroyed. No company anywhere kept them for only thirty days. I had no doubt they had been destroyed to avoid my getting them. Luckily, emails were more difficult to get rid of, as they relied on external ISPs and servers.

"All the complaints were about Herba-Cough Max?"

"Yes. It's that specific product. I don't know why, but it makes people sick, and management knew about it."

"Thank you, Ms. Ochoa. Nothing further."

Bob rose. He stared at Debbie until she looked away.

"Ms. Ochoa, how many complaints were filed against you personally by customers?"

"I don't see why that—"

"How many, ma'am?"

"Objection," I said. "I never received copies of any complaints against Ms. Ochoa."

"I'm not introducing them, Your Honor. I just want to know how many Ms. Ochoa remembers there being."

"I'll allow it."

"Your Honor," I said. "They purposely did not give me those complaints. I think it's highly—"

"Let's talk about it in chambers later," Bob interjected. "Not here."

"I agree," Hoss said. "Ms. Ochoa, you may answer."

"I don't know," she said.

"Eighty-nine. You had eighty-nine complaints filed against you by customers in a four-year period. Does that sound right?"

"I guess so."

"If you had an employee who got almost a hundred complaints in four years, would you keep that employee, Ms. Ochoa?"

"It wasn't my fault. The company wouldn't talk to any of the parents, so the parents would get mad at me and—"

"That wasn't what I asked. I asked you if you would keep an employee who had racked up a hundred complaints in four years."

"No, I guess not."

"And so when Mr. Olsen let you go, what did he tell you was the reason for your termination?"

"He said it was performance, but that's not true. I was a good employee."

"A good employee with a hundred complaints against her?"

"I told you, that wasn't my fault."

"Where did you work before Pharma-K?"

She hesitated. "An accounting firm."

"Stoole, Bobbins, and Whitman, correct?"

"Yes."

"You were terminated from that job, too. Is that not true?"

"Yes, but that was because my boss hated me. She was jealous of any women in the office."

"Before the accounting firm, you worked at a graphic design company, Hiero Graphics, correct?"

Debbie was turning red. "Yes."

"And you were fired from there, too?"

She didn't try to give an excuse this time. "Yes."

"Now, this conversation you supposedly heard, it was routine for me to come into Mr. Rucker's office and discuss issues pertaining to the company, wasn't it?"

"Yes."

"And we discussed everything about the company."

"I guess."

"So is it possible, Ms. Ochoa, that we were talking about something else? Before you got on that stand and decided to hurt a good man's reputation and the company that so generously gave you a bundle of money to make sure you were okay after they let you go, did you bother to check with me or Mr. Rucker about it?"

"No."

"And it is possible that we were talking about something else, isn't it?"

She shrugged. "Anything's possible."

"Anything's possible," he said again for emphasis. "It certainly is."

# 41

We ended the day with Debbie Ochoa's testimony. I asked the judge for a meeting in chambers. Bob and Olivia followed me back there.

I sat down across from the judge and could barely hold my anger in check.

"Your Honor, I sent a subpoena for any complaints against Ms. Ochoa, to which Mr. Walcott replied that such complaints were destroyed after termination of the employee. Everyone in this room knows that's not true. They destroyed those complaints so I couldn't contact those parents."

"Outrageous!" Bob said. "Do you know how many crazy people complain to a company like Pharma-K on a daily basis? They can't keep every single complaint against every single employee."

"They're required to keep complaints for the unemployment bene-fits process in Utah," Olivia said. "There's no way they didn't know that."

Bob chuckled. "Your Honor, these accusations are baseless. What my client does or does not do with complaints received against employees has no relevance to—"

Judge Hoss held up his hand. "Mr. Walcott, do you have these complaints in your possession at this time?"

"I do not."

"Does your client?"

"No."

"Is there any way to get them?"

"There is not. The recordings were recycled after thirty days."

The judge rubbed his forehead. "Mr. Byron is right. It doesn't seem likely that would be company policy. You either destroyed those recordings or are keeping them from him."

Bob's jaw muscles flexed. "If you have any proof, Judge, make your move."

"If I had any proof, I would be putting you in handcuffs. I'm going to give a curative instruction to the jury to disregard Ms. Ochoa's testimony regarding the number of complaints received against her. Mr. Byron, it's not much, the jury's not going to forget it, but it's all I can do unless you have a better plan."

"Tell them why," I said. "Tell them the company claims they destroy the recordings within thirty days, even though Workforce Services requires them to keep the records."

Bob shrugged. "Do what you want."

---

We began on the workers at Pharma-K the next morning. A few of them had mentioned the poisonings and were told to ignore them because it wasn't their concern, and I wanted to get those statements to the jury.

The trial had already gone on for weeks, and we weren't even to the defense witnesses yet. I had lost eighteen pounds because I wasn't sleeping or eating. Olivia had tried to force-feed me, but I wasn't hungry. The wear and tear was clear on me. Dark circles smothered my eyes, and I looked weak and pale.

On a Wednesday, we had presented every witness we had. The judge asked if I had any other witnesses. I stood up and said, "Just one, Your Honor. We would call Joel Whiting to the stand."

During the first few days of a trial, you have enough insight and energy to tell how it's going. By the second week, it's tough to tell. By the third and fourth week, you have no idea if you're winning or losing. You're just trying to get through without making too many mistakes. That's how trials are won and lost past the third week: whoever makes the least mistakes wins.

We'd made some mistakes, but overall I thought the case had gone as well as it could. The jury seemed sympathetic to Rebecca, and I don't think they believed for a second that she was just doing this for money. Still, liability was an issue. It was clear something had happened, but it was difficult to prove exactly what. If the jury thought too long about that, they would find for the defense.

Bob stood up, too. "Your Honor, again, I would renew my objection to this video. It is highly inflammatory and offers little in the way of probative value."

"I've ruled on this twice before, Mr. Walcott. I viewed the video in-camera, and you had a chance to cross-examine Mr. Whiting on video. I will allow it."

I walked to the jury and pressed Play on the television that was set up in front of them. "Joel Whiting recorded this a couple of weeks before he died."

I sat back down. The video began.

"My name . . . is Joel Whiting. I'm twelve years old, and I'm dying. People keep telling me that I can make it out of this, but I know I won't. I can tell from the way people talk to me. My friend Noah said that I should record this video if this case ever goes to trial so that you can hear what I have to say. I don't really know what to say. I just don't want any other kids to go through what I'm going through. I'm gonna miss a lot of things, and I don't want other kids to miss them, too. I don't know why I'm sick or why they can't help me, but I don't want anyone else to go through this. I want to live . . . more than anything. But if I can't, then at least I can help some other kids to."

The video went on for another eight minutes. He described taking the medication and what it felt like. He described what the hospital was like, the staff, and what the medication he was taking then felt like. The day after I'd shot my portion, Bob had come to the hospital to cross-examine Joel on video. He asked fifty useless questions in an attempt to tire the boy and get him into a rhythm of saying yes.

"That's enough, Bob," I heard myself say on the video.

"I'm not finished."

"You're being an asshole. Cut it out."

The jury chuckled.

"I am allowed to cross-examine this witness."

"You're allowed not to be an asshole, too, and I don't see you taking advantage of that."

That got another chuckle from the jury, and Bob's jaw muscles tightened.

The video ended with Joel saying, "Mom, I love you. I know I'll see you again, so I'll be good until then."

Tears streamed down Rebecca's face. I stared at a spot on the wall, unable to move. Fatigue and emotion choked me. I finally rose and turned off the video.

"The plaintiff rests, Your Honor."

———

The defense testimony on a "battle of the experts" case was the same as the plaintiff's, just in reverse. Bob put on expert after expert, and I asked essentially the same questions he had asked my experts: How much are you being paid to be here? You've never testified for the plaintiff in a civil case, have you? Do you make mistakes in your work? What was your last mistake?

I tried to challenge the credibility and motivation of each expert. Some experts were too good, and the best I could hope for was to ask a few questions, score a few points, then sit down before actually bolstering their testimony.

Olivia helped me here. I was just too exhausted to keep going. She picked up the reins and did a fantastic job cross-examining a pharmacist who stated that acetonitrile in the doses found in Herba-Cough Max wouldn't kill a boy like Joel.

"You being objective, Mr. Brail?" she asked.

"Dr. Brail, and yes."

"*Mr.* Brail, you make mistakes in your work, don't you?"

"No."

"Really? You've never made a mistake in your work as a pharmacist or as an expert for the defense?"

"Little oversights, I guess. But I know what you're asking. You're asking if my analysis could be wrong, and no, I don't believe it could."

"Approach, Your Honor?"

"You may."

Olivia flashed Bob a document that we'd downloaded from a scientific journal, and then marched to the stand. Because Olivia was using the document to impeach—to call into question the credibility of the witness—we weren't obligated to send it to Bob prior to the trial. "What is this, *Mr.* Brail?"

He looked at the document. "It's a paper I wrote ten years ago."

"A paper on vaccination for HPV, human papillomavirus infection, is that right?"

"Yes."

"Please turn to page thirty-two of that paper."

Brail sighed and turned to the page. "Yes. I'm here."

"Third paragraph, second sentence. Please read it."

"Patient twenty-six showed signs of irritation in the upper right quadrant of the vulva."

"What does that mean?"

"It means her vulva became irritated during the study."

"On the last page, I've included a list of the patients. Please tell us the name of patient twenty-six."

"Counselor, I don't know what—"

"*Mr.* Brail, please read what I asked you to read."

He rolled his eyes and flipped to the last page. His face changed. It went from the bored confidence he'd displayed during the rest of the cross, to confusion. He flipped back to another page, and then another.

"You seem concerned," Olivia said.

"It's . . . nothing big. Just a typographical error. Must be."

"Please tell us what the error is."

He glanced to Bob. "Patient twenty-six is a male."

"Last I checked, males don't have vulvas, do they?"

"No, Counselor, they don't."

"So that was a mistake, wasn't it, *Mr.* Brail?"

"Yes."

"You made a mistake."

"It's a minor oversight."

"This study was published in the *Journal of Vaccination Studies,* wasn't it? People are going to be relying on this when they make recommendations to parents about vaccinating their young girls. Yet you didn't know you'd made a mistake until I pointed it out to you." He remained quiet. "*Mr.* Brail, you wouldn't know if you've made a mistake in your analysis in this case, would you?"

"It's Dr. Brail, damn it!" he blurted out.

I grinned as Olivia sat back down next to me. I fist-bumped her when the jury wasn't looking.

The essence of the testimonies of Bob's experts was that, yes, acetonitrile had been and still was manufactured at the plant in Utah, but fool-proof procedures separated the nail polish remover from everything else. Acetonitrile could not have been mixed in with any other product. The quality-control manager of the plant was a good witness and explained, for four and a half hours, the process of the plant to ensure that substances used in one product don't leak into another.

"If an employee came to you," I said, "and told you they had tainted children's medicine with acetonitrile, you would fire that employee, wouldn't you?"

"Well, yes. We can't have someone that careless working for us."

"And if someone didn't want to get fired, the best way to assure that would be to not tell you."

He shrugged. "I couldn't say what another person would or wouldn't do."

The back-and-forth on expert cross-examination was trench warfare: each side tried to get just one more point with the jury than the other, and each point had to be clawed and fought over.

Another two weeks went by in a flash. I had accepted that I wouldn't sleep, so I drank a few tumblers of brandy before bed every night and tried to get as much rest as possible. In the morning, I had just enough energy to throw on a suit—most of the time, I wore the same one I'd worn the day before—and sluggishly make my way to court.

Olivia kept me going. When I forgot to eat, she would make a smoothie for me so I got some nutrition. When I pushed myself too far preparing for the next day, she would close my laptop and make me go outside for a walk with her. When I felt like I couldn't go on anymore, she would hold me in her arms and tell me to keep fighting. Without her, I knew I wouldn't have made it through to the second month.

Darren Rucker testified on a Friday. He was my star witness, even though I hadn't called him. If I had, I could've only used direct examination and couldn't ask leading questions, so instead, I'd let Bob call him. My plan was simple: I was going to hammer him with all 254 email customer complaints and introduce them as evidence—preferably, after he read each and every one to the jury.

"Tell us what happened when you found out about this tragedy, Mr. Rucker," Bob said to him after about thirty questions.

"I was devastated. I mean, this was the company I'd devoted my life to, and now, here were three little children who were sick because some maniac decided to use us as a murder weapon. I can't describe to you how awful I felt."

"What actions did your company take?"

"We set up a task force to deal with this immediately. We hired investigators and worked with the FDA to get everything off the shelves as fast as we could. We were open to the media, we opened our labs to the FDA and law enforcement . . . I can tell you I got very little sleep during that time. Same for the CEO, Mr. Holloway."

"You did everything you could?"

"We did everything. I don't even know how much money we spent to stop this. It felt sometimes like Mr. Holloway was willing to go bankrupt if he could save more kids from getting poisoned. We did everything we could."

Bob nodded. "Do you regret what happened?"

"What kind of question is that? Of course I regret it. If I could, I would gladly give my life to save that boy's. But life doesn't work that way. All I know is I went down to quality control after this happened and had them walk me through the process of handling acetonitrile. There is no way any of our acetonitrile got into Herba-Cough Max. It's impossible."

"Thank you," Bob said.

I stood up. "You said the first thing you did was get a task force together, right?"

"Yes."

I lifted an email off my desk and asked the judge if I could approach the witness. "What is this, Mr. Rucker?"

He looked it over. "It's an email."

"It's an email from you to your head of distribution, correct?"

"Yes."

"And it's dated April eighth, correct?"

"Yes."

"The date after this story became public."

"I guess so."

"Please read the email for the jury."

He hesitated, then began to read. "Taylor, we need to assure everyone that only Herba-Cough Max is affected. I want personal calls to all the major pharmacies and grocery chains. Assure them everything else is fine and testing clear." He handed the sheet of paper back.

"So the first thing you did was not setting up a task force, was it? It was making sure that your distributors didn't pull all your products off the shelf."

"I did a lot of things. It was a chaotic time. None of us were sleeping. We were working tirelessly to make sure everyone was safe. We even asked that all bottles of Herba-Cough Max be disposed of."

"Oh, right. You asked everyone who had Herba-Cough Max to throw it away and not use it, correct?"

"Yes. We felt that was the safest course."

"They also can't test it, can they?"

"I don't know what you mean."

"I mean, if they throw it away, those bottles can't then be tested to find out if they contained acetonitrile, can they?"

"We did it for their safety. Not because we were worried about tests."

I took out the big guns. A stack of 254 emails. I approached him slowly and stood in front of the witness box.

"How many complaints did Herba-Cough Max receive before April seventh?"

"Something like two hundred and fifty."

His honest answer surprised me, and I had to pretend to look at the pages for a moment.

"Please read this first email."

He looked at the sheet of paper, then back up at me. "No."

"Excuse me?" I said.

"I won't read it. I know what you're trying to do. You're trying to make it look like we knew about all these sick children and we still kept the medicine out there just to make money. I won't do that. This company cares about people, and I won't do that to them."

I looked to the judge. "Your Honor?"

"Mr. Rucker," the judge said, "those are exhibits that have been marked for introduction. They are part of the case. If Mr. Byron would like you to read one, please do so."

Rucker shook his head. "I won't do that. That's slimy, and I won't do it. I don't care if I go to jail. I died the day I found out about those kids. I'm not going to sit here and help you make us look like we're monsters. I won't do it."

"You had almost three hundred parents telling you your medicine made their children sick, and you did nothing about it, and you're going to sit there and be upset that I want the jury to hear it?"

"Do you know how many bottles of Herba-Cough Max we've sold? In the millions. A certain number of complaints are expected. It says on the bottle, which I don't know if you've actually read, that there may be adverse side effects because no medicine is a hundred percent safe. The multivitamins you take in the morning cause half of one percent of the population to go into anaphylactic shock. Do you expect the vitamin company to pull it off the shelves?"

"I expect them to warn me."

"We did warn them. Read the bottle. We don't know what it will do to everyone. We don't know if someone tampered with it at the stores. We don't know everything—we can't. I have children, too. You think I'd just let them take tainted medicine? Medicine is as much art as science.

It took me six years of practicing as an ER doctor to figure that out. That's why I'm working for a pharmaceutical company. We help more people every single day than I could've helped in a lifetime as a lone doctor." He shoved the emails aside. "I'm not letting you turn all our good work into another yacht for you. We save lives. What do you do, Mr. Byron? Other than robbing those who help people?"

I swallowed. My throat felt like sandpaper. My heart was beating so hard, I thought the jury could hear it. I fumbled with the papers, and a few of them fell. "I . . . um." I glanced to Rebecca. She wasn't looking at me.

I looked at the jury. They weren't on my side anymore. They were staring at Rucker as if he were someone they needed to protect from me. I sat back down. "Nothing further for this witness, Your Honor."

# 42

We sat in the conference room at the office that night—Marty, Raimi, Olivia, and I. No one said anything for a long time until Marty finally commented, "That went really bad, Noah. They were sympathizing with him. They felt bad that he had to be up there, going through this."

"We should settle," Raimi said. "They won't offer the same, but if they offer anything, we should take it."

Olivia sat upright, her back straight and her arms close to her body, as though preparing for an attack. She seemed pissed, either that we were losing, or that she had to watch me go through that. "They're still scared. Before today, it could've gone either way."

"Sorry, missy, but you're not even really an attorney here," Marty said. "I don't even know what you're doing here."

"Hey, I've done more on this case than you did."

"I'm one of the partners here. You don't speak to me that way."

I drifted off and stared out through the glass walls into the law firm.

I had lost the case. I had a sense for juries, of when they were on my side and when they weren't. That one witness had turned them against me. I rubbed my forehead. Raimi was right. We needed to settle for whatever pennies they would throw our way.

For some reason, just then, I thought of my father. I wondered if he would want to see me like this: defeated. In a way, he could never defeat me. One time, he beat me and I didn't cry. He kept hitting me, and I wouldn't respond. He stopped beating me after that. At that moment, he realized he couldn't defeat me.

No, I wouldn't let them do this. There was something . . . there was always something. Since I was a kid, I'd held an unshakeable belief that if a person wanted something bad enough, the universe would provide it. There was something in us that touched a mystery beyond ourselves . . . there had to be. Otherwise this was all for nothing.

I stared out into the firm for a good half hour while everyone argued. Then I noticed something. I glanced into the office of one of the paralegals across the hall. She had photos of her kids on her desk. Her kids . . .

"He said he has kids," I interrupted, as the three of them were arguing.

"So?" Marty said.

"Raimi, I want to send out a subpoena for Rucker's kids right now. How can I do it?"

"What?" Marty said. "That's crazy. The defense needs notice. You can't just call witnesses."

"Raimi, there's gotta be a way."

He thought for a second. "I guess if you called them as impeachment witnesses under Rule 607, the notice requirement might be waived. But they'd have to show that Rucker was untruthful on the stand. Otherwise, it's not impeachment."

"I'll draft the subpoenas. Marty, call Bob and let him know what we're doing. Get the judge on the phone in my office," I said, hurrying out of the room.

"What? What the hell are you doing, Noah?"

"Winning this case."

---

I waited in my office for the conference call. Raimi sat across from me. The phone rang, and I heard Judge Hoss's voice.

"Mr. Byron, I just received this fax stating you have subpoenaed three of Mr. Rucker's children."

"Yes, Your Honor."

"This is one of the most underhanded, disgusting schemes," Bob bellowed into the phone, "by any defense counsel I have ever worked with. To drag children into this is deplorable."

"They're impeachment witnesses, Judge. I need them to show that Mr. Rucker was untruthful today. I don't need to give notice to the defense for impeachment witnesses."

The judge said, "Mr. Walcott, what are the children's ages?"

"Eight, ten, and thirteen. Your Honor, I would demand immediate sanctions for sending those subpoenas to my client's—"

"Hold your horses, Mr. Walcott. I'm making my ruling. I'm quashing the subpoenas for the eight-year-old and ten-year-old. And shame on you for trying that, Mr. Byron. I will allow the thirteen-year-old to testify if he can show that Mr. Rucker was untruthful on the stand. If not, his entire testimony will be stricken. Mr. Walcott, can you get the boy there tomorrow?"

"I don't know, Judge."

"He's thirteen. Just write him a sick note and get him there. I don't want to keep this jury any longer than necessary."

"Yes. Fine. I'll get him there."

"Good. Mr. Byron, you have a short leash. If I feel you are abusing that boy in any way, his testimony will end."

"I understand."

"Good. I'll see you tomorrow then."

I hung up the phone and stared at Raimi. He said, "I hope you know what you're doing."

"Me, too."

# 43

I was walking into the courtroom when someone pushed me from behind. Darren Rucker stood there, his face contorted with rage.

"You cocksucker!" He stuck his finger in my face. "My kids? You're going to drag my kids into this! When this is over, I'm going to have your Bar license. Count on it."

I let him go in first, then I went and sat at the plaintiff's table with Olivia and Rebecca. The judge came out, and we all rose. He sat, booted up his computer, then said, "The plaintiff has made a request that an impeachment witness be called. I have granted that request. Please bring out the jury, and we'll proceed."

The federal marshals, who were the bailiffs in federal court, brought out the jury, and we rose again. I said, "Your Honor, the plaintiff would like to call an impeachment witness before we move on to the next defense witness. We would call Michael Rucker to the stand."

The boy was wearing a T-shirt and jeans, not a suit, and he looked as though he were about to give a talk in class without wearing pants. His eyes were wide with fear, and I could tell the jury instantly sympathized with him. I would have to be careful.

"Please state your name," I said, after he was sworn in.

"Um, Michael Rucker."

"How old are you, Michael?"

"Thirteen."

"Darren Rucker, the COO of Pharma-K Pharmaceuticals, is your father, right?"

"Yes."

I put my hands in my pockets and approached him slowly. Then I turned away and leaned against the jury box. "Michael, you've been sick before, haven't you?"

"Um, sick?"

"Yeah, you know, sick. Like with a cough and fever and all that."

"Yeah, I've been sick."

"When was the last time you were sick?"

"I don't know. Few months ago."

"How often do you get sick?"

"I don't know."

"Few times a year?"

"I guess."

I went to the plaintiff's table and picked up something I had asked Olivia to bring: a bottle of Herba-Cough Max.

"Your dad ever give you this medicine?"

"No."

"Not once. In all those times you've been sick, he never once gave you this medicine?"

"Not my dad, no."

"You ever taken this medicine?"

"Once."

He was staring at his father in the audience. I stepped between the two of them, forcing Michael to look at me. "What happened when you took it?"

"I don't know. Nothing."

I approached him. He was fidgeting. He didn't know what this was about, and I was betting Rucker hadn't told him the details. Michael didn't know what he was supposed to say. Bob either hadn't had a chance to coach his testimony, or was too scared to. Children were difficult to coach, and if asked, they would be honest as to what their preparation had been. If Bob were found to have influenced a witness's testimony in that way—something he knew I would be able to tell within the first few questions—it would be felony witness tampering. He would risk a lot for this case, but probably not prison.

"Did your mother give you the medicine the one time you took it?"

"Objection, Your Honor," Bob said. "This is irrelevant."

"Overruled," the judge said. "I'm curious to hear this as well. You may answer the question."

"Yes," Michael said.

"Just that one time?"

He nodded. "Yeah."

"Why didn't they ever give you this medicine again? Your dad works for the company. I doubt you'd have to pay for it."

"I got kinda sick."

"Sick how?"

"I was throwing up and stuff. My dad got home and told my mom to throw that medicine away. That we can never use that medicine."

My heart was in my throat; adrenaline coursed through me. "Why did he say that?"

"Your Honor!" Bob nearly shouted. "None of this has anything to do with—"

"Sit down, Mr. Walcott. Your objection is overruled."

"Go ahead, Michael. Answer the question," I said.

"He just said we were never allowed to take it because it might make us sick."

"When did he say that, Michael?"

He shrugged. "I don't know."

"What grade were you in?"

He thought a moment. "Sixth grade, I think. So, like, a year ago."

I stood next to Michael now. "Your father told you last year that you weren't allowed to take this medicine because it would make you sick?"

"Yeah." Michael nodded. He didn't even realize what he'd just said.

I turned to Bob, who stared at Rucker in turn.

Rucker got up from the audience and rushed out of the courtroom.

# 44

In the attorney–client room at the courthouse, Bob sat across from me. We had sent everyone else away; it was just the two of us.

He ran his finger across the tabletop, then grinned. "How did you know he would say that?"

"It was a shot in the dark. But I was willing to bet Rucker didn't give Pharma-K products to his own children. Yelling at me about how much they care was an act. They wouldn't put their own asses on the line."

He chuckled. "It was damn fine work. If you ever want to work for a real law firm, you should come talk to me."

"I'll pass, but thanks. Between me and you, Bob, how much did they know?"

He gazed at me. "Between me and you, Noah, the world is run by people like Rucker and people like me, who protect him. People like you just watch from the sidelines and follow our lead. It's better people like you don't know what people like us have to do to keep this world spinning."

"There's more of us than there are of you, Bob. One day, the tables will turn." I inhaled and leaned back in the chair. "I want Pharma-K to pay up."

"You could still lose, you know."

"So could you. They could give me my one fifty."

"And it'll be knocked down on appeal." He paused. "What's it going to take?"

"First," I said, "every executive involved in this has to be let go. Anyone who had anything to do with covering up the complaints can't run that company anymore. Then I want ten million for Rebecca Whiting, with an apology. I want a third-party regulator to have access to the plant and figure out how the acetonitrile leaked into the cough medicine. I also want another ten million set up in a nonprofit dedicated to Joel Whiting. I want them to focus on consumer protection, and I want an independent board in charge of choosing their officers, no one from Pharma-K. And I want the other two sick boys to get good settlements. I know closing the plant is a deal breaker, but I'm serious about full access, and I'll make sure the settlement contract reflects that."

"Twenty million to make it go away?" He nodded. "We'll do that."

"And I want an additional hundred thousand for a special project."

"What special project?"

I smiled.

---

When I stepped into the firm's office, everyone froze. They stared at me like I had just walked out of a spaceship. Finally, one person in the back, the lawyer with anchorman hair, started clapping. Then everyone else started clapping. The Commandant came up and hugged me and wouldn't let go. This case had come to symbolize something for them. I was witnessing all their worries and fears leaving their bodies. I managed to pull away from the Commandant and head to my office. Jessica saw me and started crying.

"Not you, too," I said.

"Sorry. Um . . . Tia called."

I shut the door to my office and sat. Exhaustion had eaten away at everything I had, and I felt like I needed to take a long absence and sleep eighteen hours a day. With our firm's cut of the settlement, they certainly wouldn't need me for a while. We had brought in, after expenses, six million dollars to the firm. The largest settlement we'd ever received.

I leaned my head back on the chair and stared at the ceiling. I could feel myself drifting off right then, except the adrenaline wouldn't let me. Then I remembered that Tia had called and I picked up the phone and punched in her number.

"Hey," I said as greeting.

"Rebecca called me. I can't believe what you did for her."

"It's only money."

She laughed. "Never thought I'd hear you say that."

"Never thought I'd say it. How was the wedding?"

"It's not until next week. Just going crazy planning everything. I kind of miss how we did it. Just ran off in a little chapel and didn't tell anybody. I wanted to do that again at first, but Richard's got eight siblings and said they would all freak if he didn't give a big reception and all that. I was glad. I wanted to keep that memory between just me and you."

I took a few breaths, remembering the smell of the chapel when we were married. It smelled like chrysanthemums and floor polish. "Are you happy?"

"Yeah, I think I am. Are you?"

"Getting there."

"Nothing gets you there faster than finding someone who loves you."

"I think I know that now. I'm sending you a nice gift. Tell Richard hello for me."

"I will. Thank you, Noah."

"Take care of yourself."

I hung up and only noticed then that Marty was poking his head through a crack in the door. "We come in?"

"Sure."

He and Raimi came in and sat down. The three of us looked at each other. Marty opened his mouth to say something, but no words came. He just smiled.

"I know," I said. "I know."

# 45

I went home early that night. I told the Commandant to clear my calendar, that I was taking a month off and when I got back I would take the entire firm to Mexico for a week. Fatigue had seeped into my bones and it felt like I was moving through water.

I sat on my balcony and closed my eyes, the setting sun warming my face. I heard the sliding glass door open in Jim's house and he came out and sat in one of his chairs. He lit a pipe and took a few puffs.

"You okay?" he said.

"I think I've made myself sick from work and lack of sleep, but I've never been better. You?"

"All right. Woman and I broke up. It was for the best. Wasn't the right fit."

"How do you know when it's the right fit?"

He shrugged. "I think you just know. You feel it in your guts. I been married three times and I only had that feeling once." He chuckled. "I was fourteen and she was my nanny. Don't choose who we love, though."

"What happened to her?"

"She moved back to Toronto where her family's from, and I stayed in the States. She's married and has kids now, and I'm sure she's content, but when I talk to her we both know we missed it. That person we're supposed to be with. Plato wrote that the gods were jealous of man's powers after the days of creation, that we had four arms and four legs and two heads, and were full of love and intelligence and grit, so they split us in half and threw our halves all around the earth. The point of life, then, is to find your other half and become whole again. The tragedy of life is if you find them and don't hold on."

I stared at him in the dying light of the sun. He took another pull off his pipe and then blew it out slowly through his nose.

"I'm too high. I gotta cut back on this stuff some."

"I gotta go," I said.

"Where?"

I rose, forcing every muscle to function when it didn't want to. "I'll tell you later."

---

Olivia's mother answered the door. She smiled pleasantly and said, "She's in her room."

I quietly peered into Olivia's room and saw her busy on her Mac. I leaned against the door frame and watched her, the way her fingers moved deftly across the keyboard, the muscles in her arms flexing and relaxing, the way her hair fell naturally across her shoulders and seemed to dance there every time she moved her head.

"Hi," I said.

She started, then exhaled. "Holy crap, you scared me."

"Sorry. What you working on?"

"Blog post I'm writing about this case."

I sat down on her bed. The room was too small for an adult and had only one window. I figured this was her childhood room. On the bed was a stuffed bunny, and I picked it up. "What I said before, about not becoming a lawyer . . . I was wrong. You're good at it. I was just looking at it from the wrong view. You can help a lot of people with your skills."

She rose from her desk and sat next to me. Her hand slipped into mine. "Do you know what Rebecca said to me on the way out of the courtroom? She said that Joel was smiling. You've changed the meaning of her son's death for her. With the foundation, Rebecca's gonna see that his death wasn't for nothing. I don't know of many professions where you can do something like that for people."

I tossed the bunny on the bed. "I think you and I need to talk about that foundation. It's going to need good leadership. But we can talk later. First, I'm going to give you a cut of the case. You've earned it. It will be enough to hire a full-time nurse for your mother."

"Noah—"

"No, I want to. Then, after we get the nurse and you feel comfortable, I want you to go away with me. I've taken a month off. Let's go lie on a beach in Fiji and do nothing."

She smiled, and laid her head on my shoulder. "I think that would be something worth writing another blog post about."

"Before we leave, though, we have to go to San Francisco. I have a promise to keep."

# EPILOGUE

The sun beat down on us and made me sweat. I wore a San Francisco Giants cap backward on my head as the team warmed up. The San Francisco sky was clear and blue, a perfect day.

Olivia sat next to me, wearing a Giants jersey. True to her word, she had quit our firm, but she hadn't taken a job at the ACLU. She'd been appointed in-house counsel to the Joel Whiting Foundation, a foundation set up with the express purpose to evaluate products and investigate violations of consumer-protection laws. She smiled at me as she chewed her soft pretzel.

"So what's this big surprise?"

"Look," I said, pointing to the Jumbotron with my chin and trusting that Rebecca had turned on her television at home like I had asked her to.

An image came up. It was the photo of Joel taken at the hospital, his face twisted in a ridiculous expression, the light in his eyes still innocent and full of life.

"I promised him he'd get on the Jumbotron. And I wanted him to be here for this," I said. I dipped into my pocket and came out with the small black case. Olivia saw it, and her eyes went wide and almost instantly became wet with tears. I opened it, revealing the ring inside, and said, "Will you?"

Tears rolled down her cheeks in silence as she stared at the ring. When she was able to move, she threw her arms around my neck and kissed me. The rest of the world disappeared, and I felt whole again.

# ABOUT THE AUTHOR

Photo © 2014 FotoFly Studios

Victor Methos is a former prosecutor and is currently a criminal defense attorney in the Mountain West. He is the author of over forty books and several short story and poetry collections.

After completing his undergraduate education at the University of Utah, Mr. Methos abandoned pursuing a doctorate in philosophy for law school. A partner at a law firm he helped found, he has conducted over one hundred trials and has been voted one of the most respected trial lawyers in the West by *Utah Business Magazine*.

Born in Kabul, Afghanistan, and having lived throughout the world before settling in the United States, Mr. Methos loves experiencing new cultures and peoples. His current goal is climbing the Seven Summits and hopefully not dying in the process. He divides his time between San Diego, Las Vegas, and Salt Lake City.